For
William and Oliver - LN
Harriet and Jack - PC

A Red Fox Book

Published by Random House Children's Books
20 Vauxhall Bridge Road, London SW1V 2SA

A division of The Random House Group Ltd
London Melbourne Sydney Auckland
Johannesburg and agencies throughout the world

Text copyright © Louise Nicholson, 1995, 2000
Illustrations copyright © Paul Cox, 1995, 2000

1 3 5 7 9 10 8 6 4 2

First published in Great Britain by Riverswift 1995
This revised edition published by Red Fox 2000

The right of Louise Nicholson and Paul Cox to be identified as the author
and illustrator of this work has been asserted by them in accordance with the Copyright,
Designs and Patents Act, 1988.

Printed and bound in Singapore.

THE RANDOM HOUSE GROUP Limited Reg. No. 954009

www.randomhouse.co.uk

ISBN 0 09 940327 7

LOOK OUT LONDON!

LOUISE NICHOLSON
ILLUSTRATED BY PAUL COX

HAND LETTERING BY
JUDY BALCHIN

RED FOX

CONTENTS

CONTENTS

A London Time Chart

Here are 24 London dates from the past 2,000 years. The Romans built their wall so well that some still stands. You can look for the wall, travel the route of the first underground train or visit London's first public royal park, all using the TEN BIG MAP

BC	
AD	
43	Roman Emperor Claudius invades Britain. He later sets up Londinium port and garrison and builds London Bridge.
200	The Romans build a wall around their city.
1042	Edward the Confessor, who makes Westminster his home, begins Westminster Abbey.
1066	William the Conqueror is victor at the Battle of Hastings and later builds the White Tower in the Tower of London.
1176	London Bridge is built in stone, London's only bridge until 1729.
1529	Cardinal Wolsey's fall. Henry VIII makes Whitehall Palace his main London home and Hampton Court his favourite country one.
1631	Inigo Jones designs London's first square, the Piazza in Covent Garden.
1637	Charles I opens Hyde Park, the first public royal park.
1666	Great Fire of London rages from September 2 - 5, destroying four-fifths of the City of London.
1675	Sir Christopher Wren begins the new St Paul's Cathedral.
1700s	London's population is about 575,000. It is western Europe's biggest city and twenty times the size of the next biggest English city.
1802	London is the world's largest port; great dock-building begins.
1811 - 17	Waterloo Bridge is the first of 14 bridges to be built (or rebuilt) in the nineteenth century.
1816 - 28	John Nash lays out Regent Street, Regent's Park and Regent's Canal.
1834	Palace of Westminster (Houses of Parliament) burns down; new one begun in 1835.
1837 - 74	Fourteen railway termini built, bringing workers into the capital.
1851	The Great Exhibition is held in Hyde Park; the South Kensington museums are built as a result.
1863	The world's first underground train service opens, from Paddington to King's Cross.
1890	The first Tube train runs, from King William Street to Stockwell, with electric trains in deep-level tunnels.
1922	First daily radio programmes broadcast from Savoy Hill.
1951	Festival of Britain; beginning of the South Bank centre.
1987	Docklands Light Railway and London City Airport open.
1994	Eurostar trains run from Waterloo to the Channel Tunnel.
2000	The Millennium Experience, The Tate Modern and new wings for the Science and Imperial War museums all o The Thames has a new Millennium Bridge. London's population is 7,007,000, and rising.

LOOK OUT LONDON!
Here we come!

London is a great city for children. One of the best. This book is for you, the children who want to know more about London and who want to explore it.

LONDON has one of Britain's most amazing forts, the TOWER OF LONDON. It has palaces where kings and queens lived – and BUCKINGHAM PALACE where QUEEN ELIZABETH II lives. It has the great RIVER THAMES with boats to ride on, and vast buildings such as ST PAUL'S CATHEDRAL to explore and climb.

It has so much theatre and music, street entertainment, children's museum activities and special children's places and events, that you could not possibly cover them all.

London also has huge parks right among those buildings. They have adventure playgrounds, lakes with rowing boats, ducks and birds to watch, and big open grass spaces where you can play, fly kites and picnic.

London is very old – the Romans founded it almost 2,000 years ago. And it is very big. Just getting around it is an adventure. Plenty of Londoners get lost every day!

There is nowhere quite like London. LOOK OUT LONDON! shows you how to make the most of it.

Look Out London! is your starter pack for getting to know this city and having fun in it!

PLANNING YOUR DAY

There are thousands of special events in London – almost daily arts festivals as well as traditional ones. So it is a good idea to check what will be happening in London on the days you are going out. You can begin by visiting the London Tourist Office's website at www.londontown.com. Otherwise, you'll need to visit an information centre, write for some information, make a telephone call, or buy a newspaper or magazine.

Leaflets

You can visit a LONDON TOURIST BOARD INFORMATION CENTRE The staff will have a free London information pack, lists of London events and can answer all your questions. There are also racks of leaflets. The biggest LTB centre is at Victoria Station Forecourt, London SW1, open daily 8 am - 8 pm. Other LTB centres are at Heathrow Underground Station for Terminals 1, 2 and 3, Waterloo International Railway Station, and Liverpool Street Underground station. You can also send for an LTB information pack by writing to PO Box 151, London E15 2HF.

The City of London has its own Information Centre, at St Paul's Churchyard, London EC4 (tel: 0207 332 1456) open daily April - September 9.30 am - 5 pm; October - March, Monday - Friday 9.30 am - 5 pm, Saturday 9.30 am - 12.30 pm. They publish a monthly brochure, *Events in the City of London*, listing many traditional City events and ceremonies.

By Phone

LTB runs VISITORCALL service, a recorded phone guide to London. For the full range of their information, updated daily, dial 09064 123 456 (dial 100 to check rates). The automated voice will instruct you to select subjects and press various numbers on the phone by saying, "key one", "key two" etc., so make sure you are in a quiet room and prepared with paper and pencil. KIDSLINE 0207 222 8070, gives you person-to-person advice, weekdays only.

Listings

Most national newspapers publish a selection of information on children's events in their Saturday editions. But it is best by far to buy *Time Out*, a thick magazine published every Wednesday (on sale on Tuesday in central London), which lists almost every event in London for the coming week, or *Kid's Out*, published by the *Time Out* team each month.

Half Terms & Holidays

As if there were not enough regular things to see, do and explore in London, there are always extra events whenever children are not at school.

Here are five places to check out for special holiday fun:

There will be full details in a current *Time Out*.

★ Barbican Centre
☆ South Bank Centre
★ South Kensington Museums
☆ Museum of London
★ Covent Garden Piazza

River Information

Before you take a boat up or down the Thames you will need to know when the boats go and return.

VISITORCALL has a special riverboat telephone number, 0839 123 432. To find out more about what there is to see along the banks, contact one of the following local Tourist Information Centres:

Greenwich: Pepys House, Old Royal Naval College, King William Walk, London SE10 (tel: 0870 608 2000, 0208 858 6376).

Richmond: Old Town Hall, Whittaker Avenue, Richmond, Surrey (tel: 0208 940 9125).

Southwark: 6 Tooley Street, London SE1 (tel: 0207 403 8299).

What to take with you

Although you do not want to carry much round, it is a good idea to take a few essentials. Either use your backpack or wear a jacket with large pockets. Depending on which of the BIG TEN MAPS you select, you may need a few special things, too. Here is a checklist of what you might need:

MAP of LONDON... A single-sheet map will do, but a book of maps, such as an A-Z, is better for longer trips.

SWEATER OR JACKET...... that can be tied round your neck or waist if you get hot. In winter, a pair of gloves so you are warm outside but can just stuff them in your pockets when you do not need them.

MONEY!..... Remind grown-ups not to take too much money and to keep it in a zipped bag, money belt or very deep pockets. If you are taking your pocket-money, do the same. You will need some small change, too. For instance, you need 20p pieces to use the telescopes on the Stone Gallery of St Paul's Cathedral (BIG MAP p. 22).

USEFUL CARDS...... belonging to everyone going on the expedition, eg travelcards, membership cards, discount cards, student cards, special offer leaflets.

BINOCULARS... with a strap to hang around your neck. With these you can look up at the decoration on the outside of the buildings and see further from the tops of high buildings or hills such as Greenwich Park (BIG MAP p. 19).

CAMERA...... to be photographed with a policeman, to snap your friends and family in front of your favourite building, or to catch your sister helping the magician in Covent Garden Piazza.

NOTEBOOK.... to write down interesting things you see or learn.

PAPER & A PENCIL... or crayons to draw a picture while you wait for a riverboat, or to record the things you like best in a museum.

SNACK ..... You will probably get hungry when there is no café in sight. So you may like to take an apple, a sandwich and a box of juice to keep you going.

★ ★ ★ AND LOTS OF ENERGY
That's the most important thing!

BEFORE YOU LEAVE .... it is a good idea to telephone the place you are visiting to check on any closures. If there is an entrance fee, ask if there are cheaper days or cheaper hours and if there are any discounts for families. For instance, THE MUSEUM OF LONDON (BIG MAP p. 26) entrance fee is valid for a whole year of return visits.

The London Happiness Code

★ **DO LESS AND SEE MORE.** Don't set out to do too much. It's far better to go and see one thing and explore it thoroughly. If you try to do too much, you end up spending the whole day moving from place to place.

★ **BE FLEXIBLE** If there is a long queue for what you want to see, there is usually something else nearby which is just as interesting especially in a museum.

★ **GET YOUR TIMING RIGHT** Many popular places such as the Natural History Museum can be crowded. Try going to such places the moment they open or towards the end of the day.

★ **RESPECT THE LONDON WEATHER.** If you are planning an outdoor day, always have a Plan B in case it rains!

GETTING AROUND LONDON

London has the world's largest city transport sytem. There are so many ways of travelling across, underneath or over the London roads – by taxi, by Underground or overground train, and best of all, by bus. Then there are boats up the Thames and along Regent's Canal, too.

A Taxi

which takes five people, is best used for a short journey, as it is quite expensive. The nickname for a taxi is a cab, and its driver is called a cabbie. To hail a cab, first spot one with its yellow FOR HIRE sign lit up and put your arm out. Tell the cabbie where you want to go, then hop in. The cab driver will set the meter and take the straightest route unless you ask specially to avoid traffic jams.

AMAZING·LONDON·TRAVEL·FACT ①

Every day, London buses and underground trains carry about 6·5 million passengers and cover about half a million miles.

The Underground

can be used for short journeys or for longer ones which whizz underneath crowded areas of London very quickly. It is often nicknamed the TUBE. In fact, they are two different things: the shallow Underground, which originally ran with steam trains, and the much deeper tunnels, or tubes, which opened in 1890 running electric trains. Today, all underground trains are part of the same system.

AMAZING·LONDON·TRAVEL·FACT ②

Each day, more than 460 trains carry about 2·7 million passengers along 254 miles of track (105 of them in tunnels) at an average speed of 20·5 mph, between 281 stations equipped with 64 lifts and 303 escalators.

You can take a Boat

trip on the Thames upstream or downstream from several piers (see p. 16-19). There used to be hundreds of ferry boats crossing the Thames. Today, you can take one from Tower Pier to **HMS Belfast**

and another, several miles upstream, from Ham House to Marble Hill House. Boats also go along Regent's Canal.
You can go a short way, from Paddington to Camden Lock, stopping at London Zoo. In summer, there are longer trips from Camden Lock all the way down to Limehouse Basin in the Docklands.

London has 3 systems for Trains Above Ground

Trains run from all the MAINLINE STATIONS to London's suburbs, and beyond. The NORTH LONDON LINE chugs its way from Richmond round north London and all the way down to the Docklands, where it used to deliver dock-workers. You can catch it near Kew Gardens or near Camden Lock and go up to Hampstead Heath for a hilltop run and great views. Finally, London's newest train is the DOCKLANDS LIGHT RAILWAY.

AMAZING·LONDON·TRAVEL·FACT ③

There are about 5,000 buses driving around London, stopping at 17,000 bus stops. In a year, the buses travel about 160 million miles at an average speed of 11 mph.

London by Bus

is the best fun of all. You can hop on a bus for a short journey, or clamber
upstairs and settle yourself in the front seat for a longer, gently swaying one, watching the world below you.

Q. How do we travel cheaply and avoid queueing for tickets?

A. Buy a Travelcard!

Where to buy a Travelcard

At **TRAVEL INFORMATION CENTRES** (see below), British Rail stations, all Underground stations and some local newsagents.

The Travelcard

The Travelcard works like this. It is valid for unlimited travel by Underground, British Rail, Docklands Light Railway and most buses. It is priced according to the number of zones (areas of London) included and the length of time you want it for. It can be valid for a day, a week, a month or a year. A special one-day, off-peak card covers all zones. There are also Family and Weekend Travelcards. With a Travelcard you can spend the entire day travelling all over London if you want.

A one-day Travelcard is easy to buy, but for a longer period, beware! You may need a **PHOTOCARD**. Children under 5 travel free. Children aged 5 - 15 pay child fares but need a child-rate photocard, obtainable from London Post Offices and Travel Information Centres on production of proof of age and a small photo (you can usually find a photo booth on mainline stations). Adults buying a weekly, monthly or annual card also need a photocard.

HELP !

London's transport systems are so huge that there are special **TRAVEL INFORMATION CENTRES** to help. The central one is at Victoria Station, open daily. It has free maps of bus routes and the Underground system and all information on cheap tickets. It also gives advice. Other, smaller centres are at these Underground stations: Euston, Hammersmith, King's Cross, Oxford Circus, Paddington, Piccadilly Circus, and St James's Park.

On The Move and having fun!

Here are four journeys round London that are fun in themselves......

☆ Hop on and off the number 15 bus, which travels to several of London's landmarks, including the Tower, St Paul's Cathedral, Trafalgar Square and Oxford Circus.

☆ Go to Greenwich by riverboat; return by walking through the foot tunnel to Island Gdns and taking the Docklands Light Railway to the Tower (or on to Bank).

☆ Go to Regent's Park by taking the Underground to Baker Street, enjoying a boatride on the lake and a visit to the zoo. From the north side, take a walk through the park, leaving it by canal boat to Camden Lock.

☆ Go to Hampton Court Palace by riverboat. This takes three to four hours. Return by British Rail train to Waterloo.

Official Sightseeing Tours

There are lots on offer. These are some of the best ~

☆ **THE ORIGINAL LONDON SIGHTSEEING TOUR :**
A two-hour tour (most with headphones) on an open-topped bus. No need to book – simply join at any of the 50 or so stops. Tel: 0208 877 1722 for more information and a map.

☆ **HOP ON, HOP OFF :**
Buy a ticket on the Big Bus Company's burgandy-coloured buses and hop on and off where you choose, all day long (tel: 0208 944 7810).

☆ Almost any of the **EVAN EVANS TOURS :**
Booking is essential (tel: 0208 332 2222) for London Highlights and Thames Cruise; City of London, Crown Jewels and Tower; London's West End. They also do trips out of town.

If you want to know more about London's amazing transport system, visit the **LONDON TRANSPORT MUSEUM**. It is marked on the Covent Garden **BIG MAP (p. 32 - 33)**.

HOT TIPS

Pay Less

★ Buy a Travelcard (with a photocard if necessary ~ see previous page)

★ Some museums are free; many others are free for children.

★ If a place has an entrance fee, see if a family card works out cheaper.

★ A London White Card gives discounts at many major charging museums.

PAY NOTHING

Cheaper Eats

☆ **The cheapest way to eat in London**

is to bring a picnic from home. For one thing, you will be hungry when there is no café in sight. For another, it is nice having a chew on top of a bus or on a long Underground journey (remembering always, of course, to throw your litter in the nearest rubbish bin). Plastic bottles of water are particularly useful.

✦ **You can also buy sandwiches**

from little cafés, fruit from the street markets – or something more substantial from a food store.

★ **If you have big appetites**

many restaurant chains and hotels do good hot buffets for a flat price. They usually advertise their deal in the window or outside the restaurant.

✦ **Beware of vendors**

of food, drinks and especially ice cream near a popular landmark. Prices will be much lower five minutes walk away.

Some of the best things in London are free – the National and Tate galleries, the British Museum, and all the parks. St Paul's Cathedral and Westminster Abbey have short evensong service in the afternoon, when there is often beautiful singing by the choristers (some of them as young as nine years old). Entertainers and busking musicians often perform in busy places, particularly Underground stations, subways and markets (Covent Garden is always a good place for free entertainment). There are hundreds of annual arts, sports and traditional events, many of them partly or wholly free. Here is a handful; the tourist office will provide many more:

★ CHINESE NEW YEAR, parades in Soho (January / February)

★ OXFORD AND CAMBRIDGE BOAT RACE, Putney to Mortlake (Easter Weekend)

★ EASTER SUNDAY PARADE and Harness Horse Parade (Easter Weekend)

★ COVENT GARDEN MAY FAYRE, St Paul's Churchyard (second Sunday in May)

★ GREENWICH FESTIVAL (June)

★ CITY OF LONDON FESTIVAL (July)

★ SUMMER IN THE CITY, Barbican Centre, (first week in August)

★ THAMESDAY, Waterloo to Westminster bridges (September)

★ THE LORD MAYOR'S SHOW, City. Fireworks display at the end, (November)

★ CAROL SINGING round the Christmas tree, Trafalgar Square (December)

If you are going to watch a traditional London ceremony or parade, get there in plenty of time. Policemen will often take children to the front to get the best views; they look after them carefully, and return them to the grown-ups afterwards. You could always take a plastic bucket to stand on for a better view.

'HAT'S YOU knows...

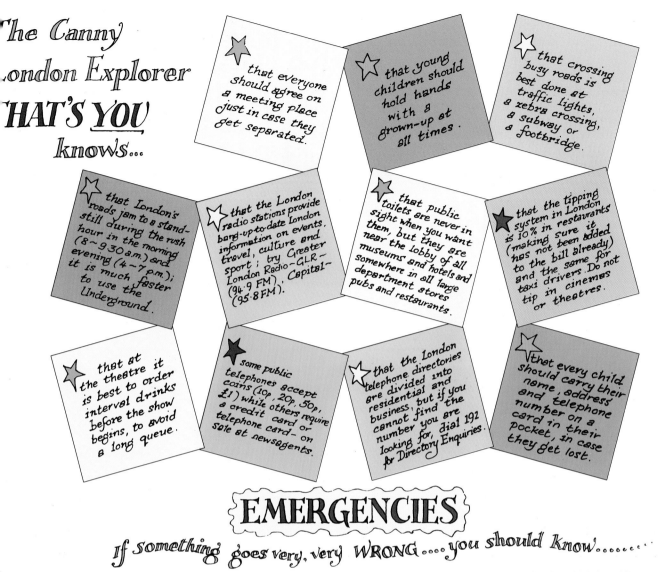

that everyone should agree on a meeting place just in case they get separated.

that young children should hold hands with a grown-up at all times.

that crossing busy roads is best done at traffic lights, a zebra crossing, a subway or a footbridge.

that London's roads jam to a stand-still during the rush hour in the morning (8~9.30 a.m.) and evening (4~7 p.m.); it is much faster to use the Underground.

that the London radio stations provide bang-up-to-date London information on events, travel, culture and sport; try Greater London Radio~GLR~ (94.9 FM), Capital~ (95.8 FM).

that public toilets are never in sight when you want them, but they are near the lobby of all museums and hotels and somewhere in all large department stores pubs and restaurants.

that the tipping system in London is 10% in restaurants (making sure it has not been added to the bill already) and the same for taxi drivers. Do not tip in cinemas or theatres.

that at the theatre it is best to order interval drinks before the show begins, to avoid a long queue.

some public telephones accept coins (10p, 20p, 50p, £1) while others require a credit card or telephone card- on sale at newsagents.

that the London telephone directories are divided into residential and business, but if you cannot find the number you are looking for, dial 192 for Directory Enquiries.

that every child should carry their name, address and telephone number on a card in their pocket, in case they get lost.

EMERGENCIES

If something goes very, very WRONG ....you should know........

that **LOST CHILDREN** can go to a policeman and will be taken to the nearest police station; in a large department store lost children are taken care of while a message is put out over the loudspeaker system.

that **LOST PROPERTY** goes to a variety of places. Lost in a taxi, it goes to the Taxi Lost Property, 15 Penton St, London, N1, lost in a train or bus, it goes to London Transport Lost Property Office, 200 Baker St, London, NW1; lost in a coach which left from or returned to Victoria Coach Station, it is kept there; lost in a Royal Park, it might be at that park's Police Station, marked on the park map.

that the telephone number for the **EMERGENCY SERVICES** is 999. No money or card is needed when you dial this number in a telephone booth. The operator will ask which service you want: police, fire brigade or ambulance. You will be connected to the one you ask for. Explain, in as few words as possible, what has happened and exactly where you are.

that central London's **LARGEST ACCIDENT AND EMERGENCY UNIT** is at University College Hospital, Grafton Way, off Gower St, London, WC1.

that Eastman Dental Hospital is at 256 Gray's Inn Rd, WC1 and has a **DENTAL EMERGENCY SERVICE**

that the Royal London **HOMEOPATHIC** Hospital is in Great Ormond St, WC1, and Ainsworth's Homeopathic Pharmacy is at 38 New Cavendish St, W1.

that Great Ormond Street **HOSPITAL FOR SICK CHILDREN** is in Great Ormond St, WC1.

LONDON AND THE THAMES

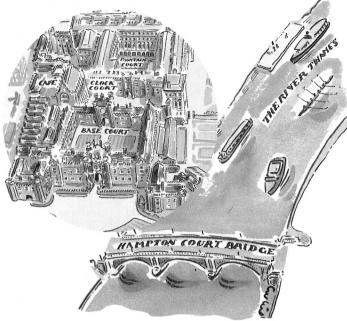

Up and Down the River

London exists because of the Thames. Soon after the Romans invaded in AD 43, Emperor Claudius founded Londinium (London) port. The Viking Danes, King Alfred and William the Conqueror followed. The port grew bigger and bigger, the merchants grew richer and richer. Ships returned home with sugar, tea, coffee, spices, jewels and with people from other countries who wanted to come to London. Within the city, the Thames was used by everyone: kings with musicians, traders, families. It was the quickest way to go almost anywhere in London.

Up the River

The upstream boat trip passes through what were once villages outside London, with fields in between them. Kings, courtiers and rich people built their country houses here to get away from the dirty city. On your trip you can hop off to walk along tow paths, run around parks or visit some of these houses and their gardens at Chiswick, Syon, Kew, Ham, Marble Hill and Hampton Court. On the **BIG MAP** over the page you can see the river twisting upstream (away from the sea) from Westminster Pier to Hampton Court, but the source of the Thames is 135 miles further west, in Gloucestershire.

Crossing the Thames

You can go over the Thames on a bridge, you can go under the Thames through a tunnel (the Greenwich Foot Tunnel is fun). There used to be steamboats, paddleboats, sailing boats, rowing boats, steaming tugs dragging barges, and ferries to cross the river. Food, people, horses - everything crossed the Thames. From the river you can see lots of landing places and stairs. Then the bridges were built. • • • • •

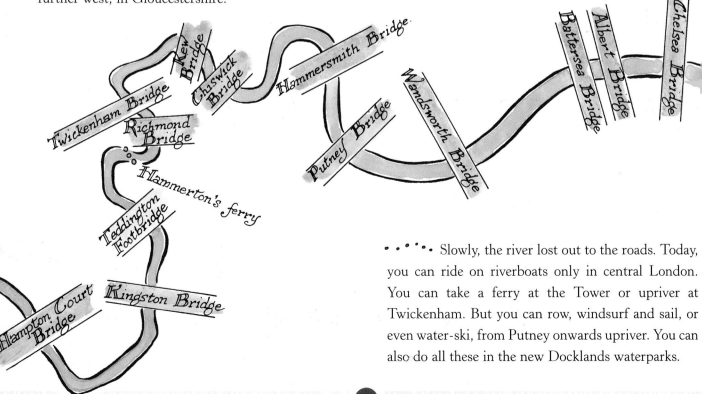

• • • • • Slowly, the river lost out to the roads. Today, you can ride on riverboats only in central London. You can take a ferry at the Tower or upriver at Twickenham. But you can row, windsurf and sail, or even water-ski, from Putney onwards upriver. You can also do all these in the new Docklands waterparks.

The Piers

It's still fun to take a boat upstream or downstream on a sunny day. Riverboats stop at more than twenty piers. Ones with lots to explore nearby include:

Hampton Court Pier
Kew Pier
Westminster Pier
British Airways London Eye Pier
Bankside Pier
Tower Pier
Greenwich Pier
Millennium Pier
Thames Barrier Pier

Down the River

The downstream boat trip passes eastwards past the City of Westminster, then the City of London and on past the old docks, which were teeming with ships until the Port moved to Tilbury about thirty five years ago. On your trip you can spot some of London's most important buildings from the river: the Houses of Parliament (right by Westminster Bridge), St Paul's Cathedral and the Tower of London. On the BIG MAP over the page you can see the Thames flowing downstream from Westminster Pier towards the sea. London is protected from the sea's storms by the world's largest movable flood barrier. Not only have the tides risen 65 centimetres over the last hundred years, but London is built on clay and is sinking slowly. Engineers used 500,000 tonnes of concrete and lots of steel to build ten gates, which can be raised quickly to block the water. There is a practice raising each month.

River Crossings

Hungerford Footbridge
Waterloo Bridge
Blackfriars Bridge
Millennium Bridge
Southwark Bridge
London Bridge
Tower Bridge
Tower Ferry
Westminster Bridge
...eth Bridge
Rotherhithe Tunnel
Greenwich Foot Tunnel
Blackwall Tunnel

TO →
Woolwich Ferry
Dartford Tunnel /
Queen Elizabeth Bridge

Fish in the Thames

There are plenty of fish in the Thames.
The seven below are amongst the most common.

Salmon   Dace   Dover Sole   Sprat   Herring   Sand Goby   Flounder

SIR JOSEPH WILLIAM BAZALGETTE

The Thames used to be much wider here. Then, 100 years ago a very clever engineer called Joseph Bazalgette made it much narrower. On the new land he laid out gardens for Londoners to enjoy. Beneath the new land he put an underground train so people could avoid the traffic, and a huge sewer to stop London smelling so much — until then all dirty water went straight into the Thames. It was called the 'Great Stink'!

CITY OF LONDON

WESTMINSTER

ST PAUL'S CATHEDRAL
MUSEUM OF LONDON
THE TEMPLE
BLACKFRIARS
MANSION HOUSE
CANNON STREET
TOWER HILL PAGEANT
TOWER OF L.
COURTAULD GALLERIES
TEMPLE
TEMPLE GARDENS
BLACKFRIARS BR.
CITY OF LONDON GRIFFIN
MILLENNIUM BRIDGE
BANKSIDE PIER
SOUTHWARK BRIDGE
SCHOONER KATHLEEN MAY
TOWER PIER
HMS BELFAST
TOWER BRIDGE
EMBANKMENT
EMBANKMENT PIER
WATERLOO BRIDGE
TATE MODERN
SHAKESPEARE GLOBE
MUSEUM
LONDON BR.
LONDON BRIDGE
HAY'S GALLERY
SKYLINE MILLENNIUM BALLOON
SOUTHWARK CATHEDRAL

HUNGERFORD BRIDGE
PIER BANDSTAND LONDON EYE
EMBANKMENT GARDENS
ROYAL FESTIVAL HALL
HAYWARD GALLERY
NATIONAL THEATRE
LONDON IMAX
WESTMINSTER
BOUDICCA
WESTMINSTER PIER
JUBILEE GARDENS
WATERLOO
THE LONDON AQUARIUM
SOUTHWARK
WESTMINSTER BR.
HOUSES OF PARLIAMENT

SOUTHWARK

When you visit the Tower, you can take a ferry from Tower Pier across to see HMS Belfast with sailors' rooms, weapons and plenty of ladders to climb...... after that, the London Dungeon is a scary selection of witchcraft, torture and horrors which all used to happen in London – You need to be very brave to come here.

The South Bank is a giant Thameside entertainment strip. Can you count how many different places there are to explore?

The best riverside walk in Central London is between Westminster Bridge and Tower Bridge. Here are four things to look out for ~
1. ~ The Statue of Queen Boudicca on Westminster Bridge. She is driving her chariot from London after she burnt it to the ground when the Romans were living here.
2. ~ The Neon Tower on top of the Hayward Gallery. The wind makes its strips of colour change – it is difficult to stop watching.
3. ~ London Bridge. The Romans built the first of many London Bridges of wood. They often burnt down or were even blown away – hence the nursery rhyme "London Bridge is falling down".
4. ~ Cleopatra's Needle, on the north bank, is London's oldest monument. The 28-metre tall granite obelisk was made in 1450 BC to celebrate Rameses the Great.

H.M.S. BELFAST

Tower Bridge has a museum on top and a road below which opens for tall ships.

ARCHBISHOP'S PARK
VICTORIA TOWER GARDENS
TATE BRITAIN
LAMBETH BRIDGE
LAMBETH PALACE
VAUXHALL BRIDGE
LONDON BALLOON CO
IMPERIAL WAR MUSEUM
LAMBETH
KENNINGTON

THE LONDON DUNGEON

VAUXHALL

To look down on London from above, take a ride in the British Airways London Eye (BALE), the Skyline Millennium Balloon, or the London Balloon Co's balloon.

Q. Who owns the swans swimming in the Thames?

QUEEN BOUDICCA

SHAKESPEARE'S GLOBE

NONESUCH HOUSE

OLD LONDON BRIDGE

A. The Queen and the Guilds of course, called Swan - upping. Twice for Vintners and not

18

THE RIVER THAMES
FROM WANDSWORTH TO WOOLWICH

LONDON BRIDGE

Until 1729 only one bridge spanned the Thames in London. That was London Bridge. The next was Putney Bridge. How many bridges can you count now? Some are for cars, some for trains and three are just for people. One of the best places to plot out London is from Waterloo Bridge: east towards the City and south-west towards Westminster.

The Thames twists so much that a good trick is to ask people which direction the boat is moving in. Going up river they will probably say west, but there will be moments when it is east, north or south.

The drivers of the riverboats which go upstream and downstream from Westminster Pier will point out things to see. It is a good idea to bring a pair of binoculars.

Christopher Wren, who designed St Paul's Cathedral, was the architect of the Royal Hospital where old soldiers live.

PIMLICO

CHELSEA HOSPITAL

RANELAGH GARDENS

CHELSEA PHYSIC GARDEN

CHELSEA OLD CHURCH

CHELSEA BRIDGE

GROSVENOR BR.

BATTERSEA BR.

ALBERT BR.

PEACE PAGODA

BATTERSEA POWER STATION

Battersea park was built for London people when the huge Victoria Docks were being dug out. Boatloads of earth were brought from there to fill in this marshy land.

CHELSEA

BATTERSEA PARK

BATTERSEA

Watch out for herons and cormorants hunting Thames fish. The river is home to more than 100 kinds of fish including all those painted in the margins of these pages.

CHELSEA HARBOUR

CHELSEA HARBOUR PIER

WANDSWORTH BR.

FULHAM

HURLINGHAM HOUSE SPORTS CLUB

It is a bad idea to swim in the Thames, although Charles II used to swim in it often.

SWAN-UPPING

Dyers and Vintners (wine sellers). During the annual the new cygnets' beaks are nicked once for Dyers, at all for the Queen.

WANDSWORTH

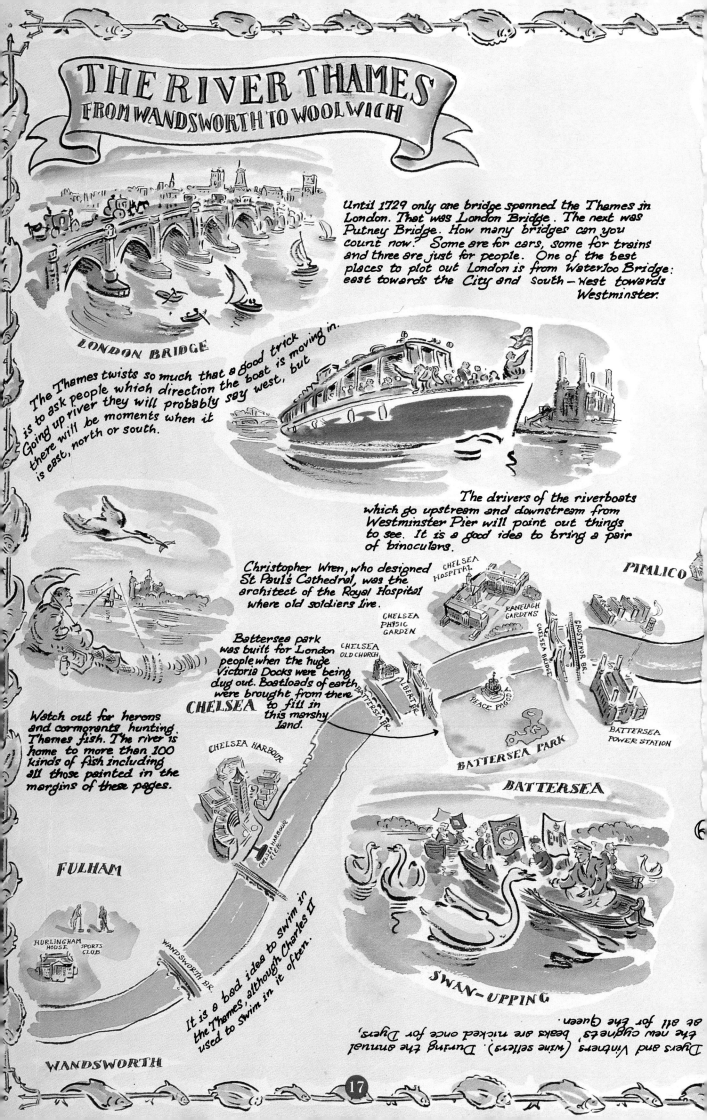

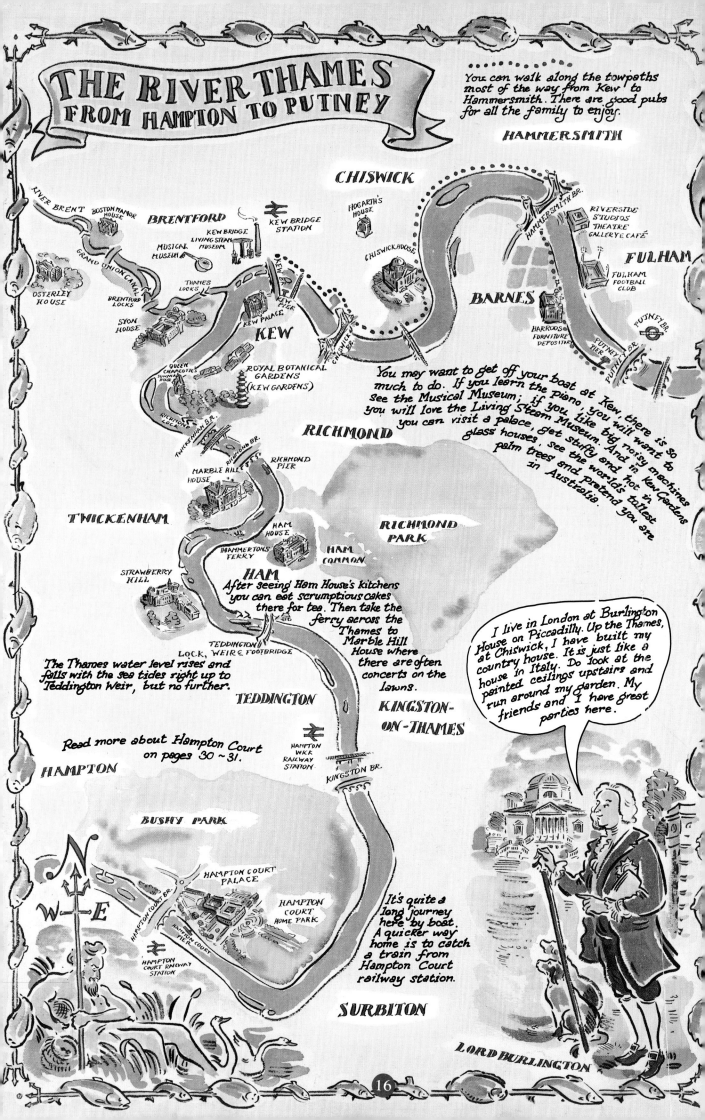

Katharine's Dock is a good [pla]ce to go for a safe run around [and] some food after visiting [the] Tower. It's fun watching [the] yachts go through the locks.

If you take the riverboat to Greenwich you could come back by walking under the Thames through the Foot Tunnel. The high-level Docklands Light Railway whizzes over the old docks past the 250-metre-high Canary Wharf Tower and back to Bank station in the City.

The Millennium Dome is so big that 13 Albert Halls could fit inside, and each bright yellow mast is twice the length of Nelson's Column. Inside, interactive displays follow the theme of time. The dome is part of the Millennium Experience ~ remember to buy your ticket before you go there.

[News] International prints more than [a mil]lion newspapers here every day.

[I] was born here at [Gr]eenwich and this is my [favou]rite palace. I can watch the [ship]s coming past to London port, and [I] go hawking or jousting in my [pa]rk. If I'm bored I just go to [a]nother palace by boat ~ Whitehall or Hampton Court perhaps.

If you stand astride The Greenwich Meridian at Flamsteed House, one foot will be in the western hemisphere and the other in the eastern. The line marks zero degrees longitude, and the whole world's time is measured from here.

There is lots to see and do at Greenwich. Do not miss Gypsy Moth IV, the little boat Sir Francis Chichester sailed round the whole world in. In the museum there are beautiful barges that kings rode in. At 1 pm you can see the Time-Ball drop on Flamsteed House to tell passing sailors the time ~ Can you spot St Paul's Cathedral from the Terrace high in the park?

LIMEHOUSE
GRAND UNION CANAL
RIVER LEA
LIMEHOUSE CUT
[DOCK]LANDS LIGHT RAILWAY
SHADWELL
[SH]ADWELL
[NE]WS INTERNATIONAL
[WAP]PING [MAPPING]
ROTHERHITHE TUNNEL
ECOLOGICAL PARK
KING STAIRS GARDEN
[BER]MONDSEY
[Ber]mondsey
SOUTHWARK PARK
ROTHERHITHE
LIMEHOUSE BASIN
LIMEHOUSE
POPLAR
CANARY WHARF TOWER
CANARY WHARF
SOUTH QUAY
ISLE OF DOGS
CUBITT TOWN
MILLWALL PARK
MILLWALL
ISLAND GARDENS
FOOT TUNNEL
DEPTFORD
DEPTFORD CREEK
GREENWICH PIER
GYPSY MOTH
CUTTY SARK
NATIONAL MARITIME MUSEUM
GREENWICH MERIDIAN LINE
QUEEN'S HOUSE
FLAMSTEED HOUSE
RANGERS' HOUSE
GREENWICH
OLD NAVAL COLLEGE
GREENWICH PARK
THE ROYAL OBSERVATORY
GREENWICH PLANETARIUM
TERRACE
[L]EAMOUTH
BLACKWALL TUNNEL
MILLENNIUM PIER
SKYSCAPE
MILLENNIUM DOME
NORTH GREENWICH
GREENWICH PENINSULA
CANNING TOWN
LONDON CITY AIRPORT
ROYAL VICTORIA DOCK
To the Sea
THAMESBARRIER PIER
THAMES FLOOD BARRIER
THAMES BARRIER MUSEUM
WOOLWICH

HENRY VIII

GREENWICH

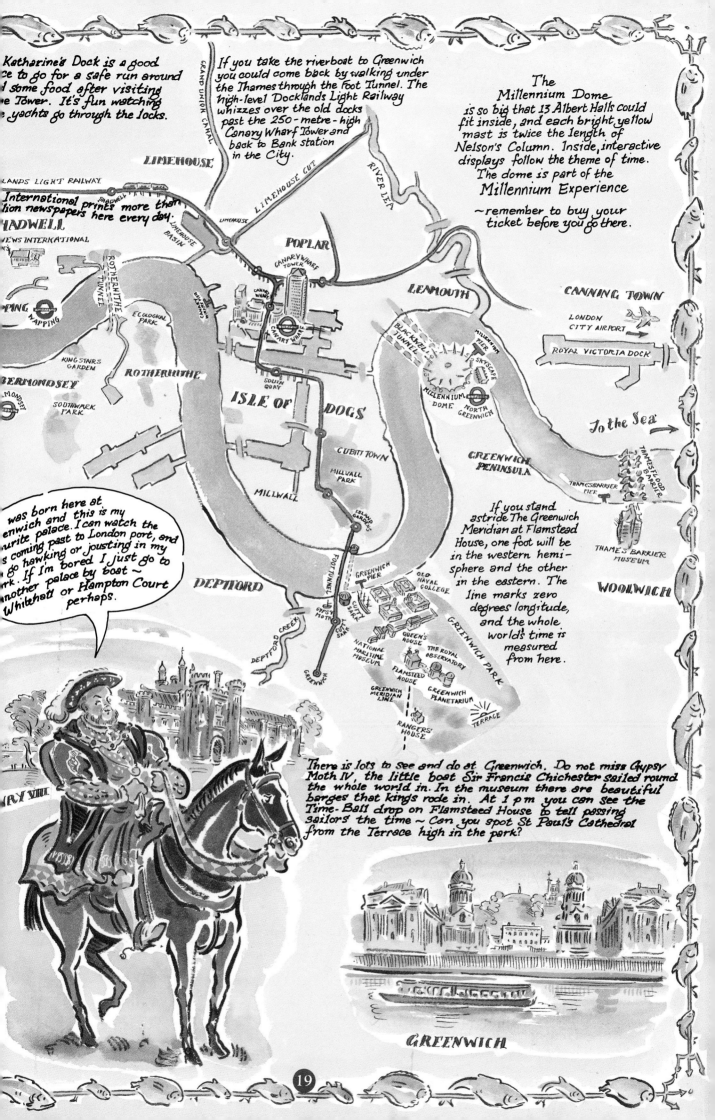

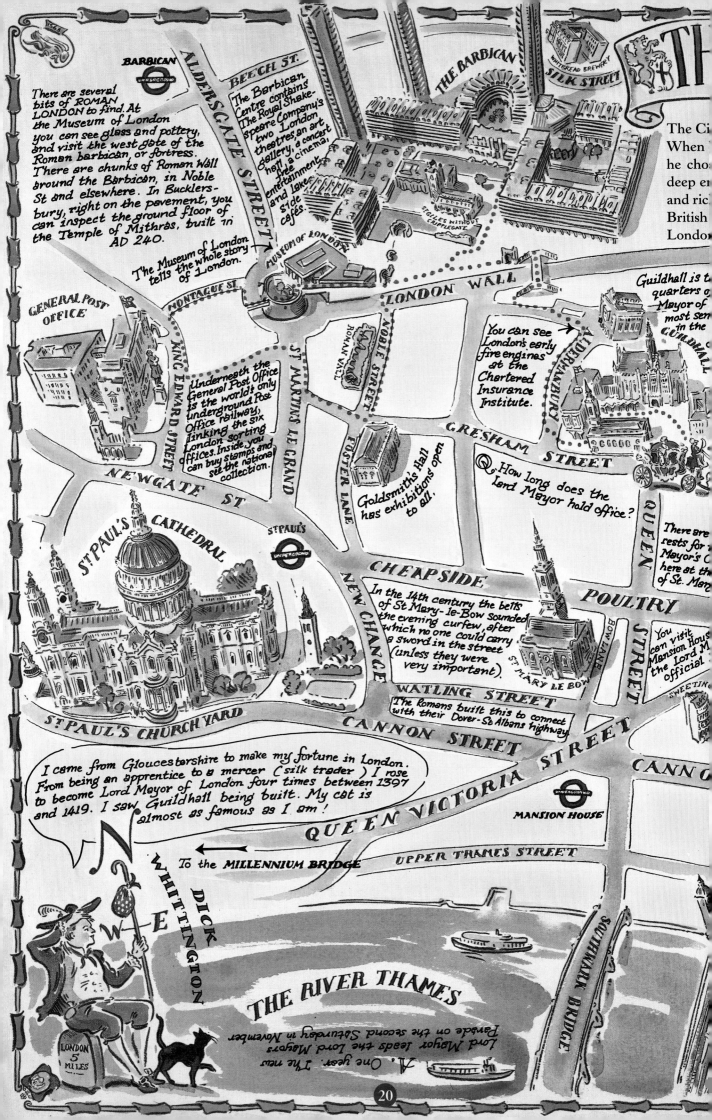

There are several bits of ROMAN LONDON to find. At the Museum of London you can see glass and pottery, and visit the west gate of the Roman barbican, or fortress. There are chunks of Roman Wall around the Barbican, in Noble St and elsewhere. In Bucklersbury, right on the pavement, you can inspect the ground floor of the Temple of Mithras, built in AD 240.

BARBICAN UNDERGROUND

ALDERSGATE STREET

BEECH ST.

The Barbican Centre contains The Royal Shakespeare Company's two London theatres, an art gallery, a concert hall, a cinema, free entertainment and lakeside cafés.

THE BARBICAN

SILK STREET

WHITBREAD BREWERY

The Ci
When
he cho
deep e
and ric
British
London

The Museum of London tells the whole story of London.

MUSEUM OF LONDON

ST GILES WITHOUT CRIPPLEGATE

LONDON WALL

GENERAL POST OFFICE

MONTAGUE ST.

KING EDWARD STREET

ST MARTINS LE GRAND

NOBLE STREET

ROMAN WALL

You can see London's early fire engines at the Chartered Insurance Institute.

ALDERMANBURY

Guildhall is t
quarters o
Mayor of
most sen
in the
GUILDHALL

Underneath the General Post Office is the world's only underground Post Office railway, linking the six London sorting offices. Inside you can buy stamps and see the national collection.

NEWGATE ST

FOSTER LANE

GRESHAM STREET

Goldsmiths Hall has exhibitions open to all.

Q. How long does the Lord Mayor hold office?

ST PAUL'S CATHEDRAL

ST PAUL'S UNDERGROUND

CHEAPSIDE

POULTRY

There are
rests for
Mayor's C
here at the
of St. Mar

In the 14th century the bells of St Mary-le-Bow sounded the evening curfew, after which no one could carry a sword in the street (unless they were very important).

ST MARY LE BOW

BOW LANE

QUEEN STREET

You can visit Mansion Hous the Lord M official

NEW CHANGE

ST PAUL'S CHURCH YARD

WATLING STREET
The Romans built this to connect with their Dover-St Albans highway

CANNON STREET

SWEETIN

I came from Gloucestershire to make my fortune in London. From being an apprentice to a mercer (silk trader) I rose to become Lord Mayor of London four times between 1397 and 1419. I saw Guildhall being built. My cat is almost as famous as I am!

QUEEN VICTORIA STREET

CANN

MANSION HOUSE UNDERGROUND

To the MILLENNIUM BRIDGE

UPPER THAMES STREET

N
W E
S

DICK WHITTINGTON

SOUTHWARK BRIDGE

THE RIVER THAMES

LONDON 5 MILES

A. One year. The new Lord Mayor leads the Lord Mayors Parade on the second Saturday in November

CITY OF LONDON

Sun or rain

where London began.
...ius founded London in AD 43
...ause the tidal Thames waters were
... London became England's biggest
...urope's, then capital of the enormous
...the City is still the financial centre of
...e to start exploring it is the Museum
... of London, then follow the dots.

Sit here in one of the cafés around the Arena to watch the free week-day entertainment.

BROADGATE

LIVERPOOL ST. STATION

UNDERGROUND

LIVERPOOL STREET

LONDON WALL

The Nat West Tower was completed in 1981. It is 200 metres high, has foundations 35 metres deep and sways with the wind. The ground plan is in the shape of the bank's logo, a permanent advertisement to airline passengers.

...e Bank of England, founded in ...4, is at the head of more than 500 banks with offices in London. It has a free museum ...garet Lothbury where you can learn all about money (without spending any.)

THROGMORTON

THE STOCK EXCHANGE

NAT WEST TOWER

OLD BROAD ST.

BISHOPSGATE

HOUNDSDITCH

CAMOMILE ST.

To The East End & Petticoat Lane Market

THE LONDON DETECTIVE
follow the dots

With lots of narrow lanes crammed into a safe small area, the City of London is a good place to **PLAY DETECTIVE**. Just choose your walk and dip down side lanes. You can **SEARCH FOR** chunks of Roman wall. You can try to **WORK OUT** what went on in the little lanes by reading their names. 'Cheape' means market, and the lanes in Cheapside include Wood, Milk, Bread, Grocers and Friday (for fish).

You can **LOOK OUT FOR** the magnificent halls built by the guilds of craftsmen founded to keep up the standards and look after their members. Goldsmiths' Hall, one of the grandest, is often open to the public.

You can **EXPLORE** inside some of Sir Christopher Wren's churches and find places for putting swords, flags and even pet dogs.

You can **SEE HOW** the city works at Guildhall and the Bank of England Museum, and **EAT** with city workers in Sweetings in Queen Victoria St.

BANK OF ENGLAND

...THBURY

THREADNEEDLE ST.

WELLINGTON

CORNHILL

GRACECHURCH STREET

LEADENHALL STREET

LEADENHALL MARKET

LLOYD'S BUILDING

...HOUSE

UNDERGROUND BANK

ST. MARY WOOLNOTH

SIMPSONS

LOMBARD ST.

Beautiful banking signs show this was where the Italian bankers (the Lombards) worked.

ST. MARY ...KING ...CHURCH

WILLIAM ST.

...REET

Look for the gilded pelican and kennels for pet dogs next to the pews in Wren church of St Mary Abchurch.

FENCHURCH STREET

The diary-writer Pepys watched the Great Fire rage for four days from the steeple of All Hallows church. In the church crypt there is a Roman pavement. See how high London has risen since then.

EAST CHEAP

MONUMENT

GREAT TOWER ST.

You can climb the 300 dark spiral stairs of Monument. It commemorates the Great Fire of 1666 which began here in Pudding Lane

THE MONUMENT

OLD BILLINGSGATE FISH MARKET

BYWARD ST.

ALL HALLOWS BY-THE-TOWER

TOWER HILL

THE TOWER ... LONDON

UPPER THAMES STREET

LONDON BRIDGE

LOWER THAMES ST.

HMS BELFAST

TOWER BRIDGE

ST PAUL'S CATHEDRAL

Eight piers made of Portland stone support the dome. The pieces of stone were brought by boat from Dorset along the coast and up the Thames, then hauled up the narrow London lanes.

The dome is the second largest in the world and weighs about 65,000,000 kilos. There are in fact three domes: one outside, one inside and one in between to hold up the lantern and cross which weigh 711,200 kilos.

St Paul's

Sun or rain

If you climb up to the Golden Gallery you have gone up 650 steps and will have a very good view of London ~ even if your legs hurt.

If you reach the outdoor Stone Gallery you will need 20p pieces to use the telescopes.

NEW CHANGE

NEWGATE STREET

St PAUL'S

If you walk up the easy steps to the Whispering Gallery, which runs around the inside of the dome, make a whisper right beside the wall and it will be heard clearly the other side of the dome.

At 1pm every day you can hear Great Paul, the largest swinging bell in Europe, being rung for five minutes. It hangs in the South Tower.

CHOIR

QUEEN ANN

N

St PAUL'S CHURCHYARD

Ⓐ You can go down into the crypt here.

Ⓑ Stand right beneath the dome and look up into it to feel the vast size of St Paul's.

Ⓒ This is where you go up to the galleries.

ST. PAUL'S CATHEDRAL

St Paul is London's patron saint. The first St Paul's, built in 604, was made of wood and later burned down. So did the second, third and fourth. This one is built of stone. It is the first English cathedral to be built by one architect and the only one with a dome. The architect was Sir Christopher Wren. His dome, best seen from the Whispering Gallery, is filled with paintings of the life of St Paul.

All sorts of British people are buried or remembered in St Paul's, but no kings – they are in Westminster Abbey. There are memorials to Florence Nightingale the nurse, John Donne the poet, Nelson the sailor hero, and many more.

St Paul's is so big that 130 people are employed full time to keep it running smoothly. They include choristers, plumbers, stonemasons, electricians, librarians, and organists to play the great organ.

The cross of St Paul's Cathedral is 111 metres above ground level.

THE DUKE OF WELLINGTON MEMORIAL

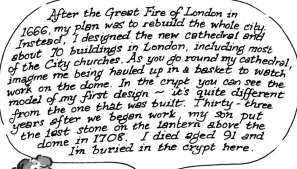

After the Great Fire of London in 1666, my plan was to rebuild the whole city. Instead, I designed the new cathedral and about 70 buildings in London, including most of the City churches. As you go round my cathedral, imagine me being hauled up in a basket to watch work on the dome. In the crypt you can see the model of my first design ~ it's quite different from the one that was built. Thirty-three years after we began work, my son put the last stone on the lantern above the dome in 1708. I died aged 91 and I'm buried in the crypt here.

In the nave look for the huge memorial to the DUKE OF WELLINGTON. He is there on top, riding his favourite horse ~ Copenhagen.

Queen Victoria thought St Paul's was dull, so mosaics (pictures made of tiny pieces of coloured glass) were added. The ones in the choir domes show living things created by God. Look for the hippopotamus and the elephant.

As with all churches, the building of St Paul's was begun from the east, where the altar is, continued through the choir and nave and finished in the west, where the grandest entrance is.

SIR CHRISTOPHER WREN

Q. Who paid for St Paul's Cathedral?

A. The people of London, who paid a special tax on coal brought into London port.

THE TOWER OF LONDON

The Tower of London is Britain's best medieval fortress. It was originally built so that William I (William the Conqueror) could keep a fierce watch over the unruly London merchants and their port while he lived up at Westminster. During its 900 years it has been fortress, treasury, palace, notorious prison, armoury, zoo, royal mint and execution site – sometimes all at once. There is so much to see – go early.

There are 42 Yeoman Wardens who guard the Tower and each night lock the gates. Their blue or red Tudor uniforms are the same as those worn by Henry VII's bodyguard, who were nicknamed Beefeaters. Do not miss their tours from Byward Tower.

If you arrive by boat, think of Elizabeth I, who arrived this way as a prisoner when she was a princess. Unlike her mother, Anne Boleyn, she was freed.

The White Tower

William I built this part, with walls five metres thick. The one door is high up with a removable staircase for times of siege. Inside, the anti-clockwise staircase allowed the king's soldiers to fight with their sword-hands free as they went down. Today, the Museum of the Tower of London is here.

Can you find the beheading block and the axe? Terrible tortures have been inflicted on prisoners here. Some were stretched on the rack, others crushed between iron hoops until they bled.

The Crown Jewels

The Imperial State Crown, **The Imperial Mantle** and the world's largest diamond, **The Star of Africa**, are part of THE CROWN JEWELS kept in the Jewel House.

Eight ravens live by the Wakefield Tower and guard the Tower of London. Some people believe that if the ravens leave, the Tower and the monarchy will fall. Protected by royal decree, they are looked after by the Ravenmaster. Watch out, they may attack strangers!

The Tower of London is the city's smallest village. Forty-three families live here.

Losing your Head

To be executed inside the Tower was considered a privilege. Anne Boleyn was beheaded here on Tower Green. Most executions took place on Tower Hill. Crowds of people came to watch for fun. When the Duke of Monmouth was still alive after five chops of the axe, his executioner used a knife to finish him off.

The Bloody Tower is where the "little princes" – the boy-king Edward V and his younger brother – were murdered after their uncle, Richard III, had made himself king.

Around and About the Tower

TOWER BRIDGE, opened in 1894, is London's last bridge before the Thames Barrier and the only bridge which can be raised (and often is). TOWER BRIDGE MUSEUM is partly on top of the bridge, partly at the far end. The river walk leads to the DESIGN MUSEUM and the TEA AND COFEEE MUSEUM. From TOWER PIER you can catch a ferry to HMS BELFAST and walk to THE LONDON DUNGEON. This is also a good moment to take a RIVERBOAT or the Docklands Light Railway to GREENWICH.

Q. What is a Scavenger's Daughter?

A. A torture instrument which crushes its victims.

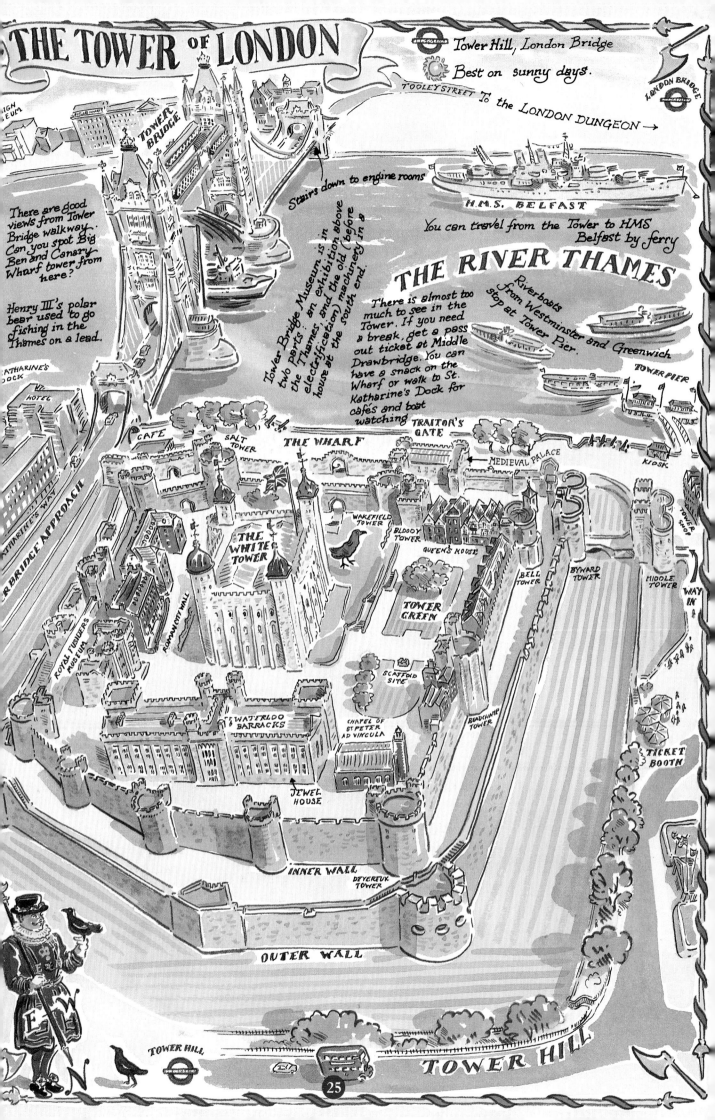

THE TOWER OF LONDON

Tower Hill, London Bridge

Best on sunny days.

TOOLEY STREET To the LONDON DUNGEON →

LONDON BRIDGE

Stairs down to engine rooms

H.M.S. BELFAST

You can travel from the Tower to HMS Belfast by ferry

There are good views from Tower Bridge walkway. Can you spot Big Ben and Canary Wharf tower from here?

Henry III's polar bear used to go fishing in the Thames on a lead.

Tower Bridge Museum is in two parts: an exhibition above the Thames; and the old (before electrification) machinery in a house at the south end.

THE RIVER THAMES

Riverboats from Westminster and Greenwich stop at Tower Pier.

There is almost too much to see in the Tower. If you need a break, get a pass out ticket at Middle Drawbridge. You can have a snack on the Wharf or walk to St. Katharine's Dock for cafés and boat watching.

TOWER PIER

KIOSK

TRAITOR'S GATE

THE WHARF

MEDIEVAL PALACE

CAFE

SALT TOWER

KATHARINE'S DOCK

HOTEL

WAKEFIELD TOWER

BLOODY TOWER

QUEEN'S HOUSE

THE WHITE TOWER

TOWER GREEN

BELL TOWER

BYWARD TOWER

MIDDLE TOWER

TOWER SHOP

WAY IN

ROMAN CITY WALL

ROYAL FUSILIERS MUSEUM

SCAFFOLD SITE

TICKET BOOTH

WATERLOO BARRACKS

CHAPEL OF ST PETER AD VINCULA

BEAUCHAMP TOWER

JEWEL HOUSE

INNER WALL

DEVEREUX TOWER

OUTER WALL

TOWER HILL

TOWER HILL

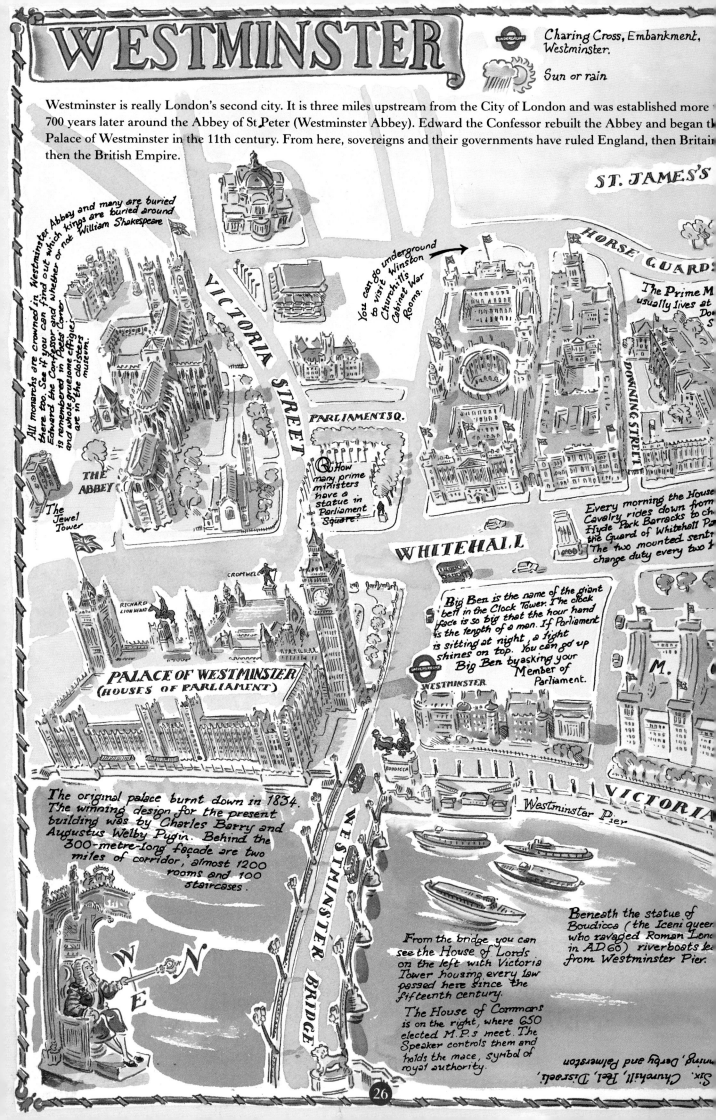

WESTMINSTER

Charing Cross, Embankment, Westminster.

Sun or rain

Westminster is really London's second city. It is three miles upstream from the City of London and was established more 700 years later around the Abbey of St Peter (Westminster Abbey). Edward the Confessor rebuilt the Abbey and began th Palace of Westminster in the 11th century. From here, sovereigns and their governments have ruled England, then Britain then the British Empire.

ST. JAMES'S

HORSE GUARDS

All monarchs are crowned in Westminster Abbey and many are buried there too. See if you can find out which kings are buried around Edward the Confessor and whether or not William Shakespeare is remembered in Poets Corner and whose gruesome effigies are in the cloisters museum.

You can go underground to visit Winston Churchills Cabinet War Rooms.

The Prime M usually lives at Do S

THE ABBEY

The Jewel Tower

VICTORIA STREET

PARLIAMENT SQ.

Q. How many prime ministers have a statue in Parliament Square?

WHITEHALL

Every morning the House Cavalry rides down from Hyde Park Barracks to ch the Guard of Whitehall Pa The two mounted sentr change duty every two h

CROMWELL

RICHARD LION HEART

Big Ben is the name of the giant bell in the Clock Tower. The clock face is so big that the hour hand is the length of a man. If Parliament is sitting at night a light shines on top. You can go up Big Ben by asking your Member of Parliament.

WESTMINSTER

M.

PALACE OF WESTMINSTER (HOUSES OF PARLIAMENT)

BOUDICCA

VICTORIA

Westminster Pier

The original palace burnt down in 1834. The winning design for the present building was by Charles Barry and Augustus Welby Pugin. Behind the 300-metre-long façade are two miles of corridor, almost 1200 rooms and 100 staircases.

WESTMINSTER BRIDGE

W N S E

From the bridge you can see the House of Lords on the left with Victoria Tower housing every law passed here since the fifteenth century.

The House of Commons is on the right, where 650 elected M.P.s meet. The Speaker controls them and holds the mace, symbol of royal authority.

Beneath the statue of Boudicca (the Iceni queer who ravaged Roman Lond in A.D.60) riverboats lea from Westminster Pier.

Six, Churchill, Peel, Disraeli, ning, Derby and Palmerston

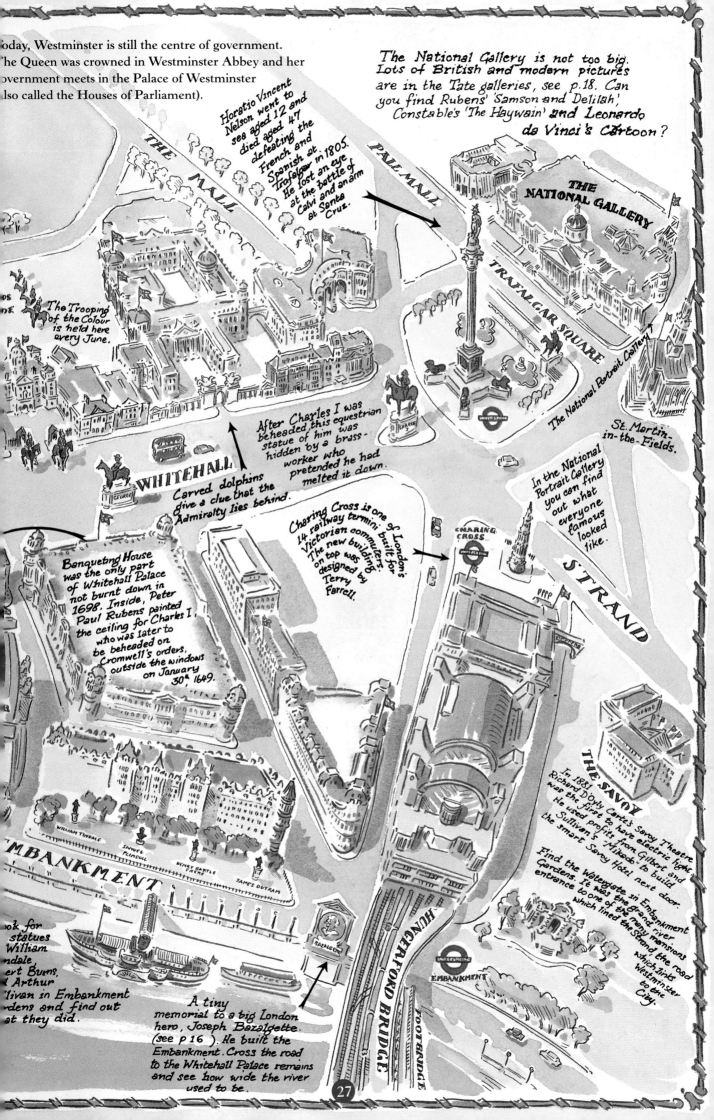

Today, Westminster is still the centre of government. The Queen was crowned in Westminster Abbey and her government meets in the Palace of Westminster (also called the Houses of Parliament).

The National Gallery is not too big. Lots of British and modern pictures are in the Tate galleries, see p.18. Can you find Rubens' 'Samson and Delilah', Constable's 'The Haywain' and Leonardo da Vinci's Cartoon?

Horatio Vincent Nelson went to sea aged 12 and died aged 47 defeating the French and Spanish at Trafalgar in 1805. He lost an eye at the battle of Calvi and an arm at Santa Cruz.

THE MALL

THE NATIONAL GALLERY

PALL MALL

TRAFALGAR SQUARE

The Trooping of the Colour is held here every June.

The National Portrait Gallery

St. Martin-in-the-Fields.

WHITEHALL

After Charles I was beheaded, this equestrian statue of him was hidden by a brassworker who pretended he had melted it down.

Carved dolphins give a clue that the Admiralty lies behind.

Charing Cross is one of London's 14 railway termini, built for Victorian commuters. The new building on top was designed by Terry Farrell.

In the National Portrait Gallery you can find out what everyone famous looked like.

CHARING CROSS

STRAND

Banqueting House was the only part of Whitehall Palace not burnt down in 1698. Inside, Peter Paul Rubens painted the ceiling for Charles I who was later to be beheaded on Cromwell's orders, outside the windows on January 30th 1649.

THE SAVOY

In 1881 Richard D'Oyly Carte's Savoy Theatre was the first to have electric light. He used profits from Gilbert and Sullivan's 'Mikado' to build the smart Savoy Hotel next door.

Find the Watergate in Embankment Gardens. It was the grand river entrance to one of the many mansions which lined the Strand, the road which links Westminster to the City.

EMBANKMENT

WILLIAM TINDALE

SAMUEL PLIMSOLL

HENRY BARTLE FRERE

JAMES OUTRAM

...ook for ...statues ...William ...ndale ...rt Burns ...Arthur ...livan in Embankment ...rdens and find out ...t they did.

A tiny memorial to a big London hero, Joseph Bazalgette (see p 16). He built the Embankment. Cross the road to the Whitehall Palace remains and see how wide the river used to be.

BAZALGETTE

UNDERGROUND

EMBANKMENT

HUNGERFORD BRIDGE

FOOTBRIDGE

BUCKINGHAM PALACE

St. Jamess Park
Victoria
Hyde Park Corner

Best on Sunny days

THE ROYAL MEWS

The State Rooms overlook the gardens where the Queen walks her corgi dogs and holds her garden parties.

PICCADILLY

GREEN PARK

Handel's "Fireworks" music was first performed at a favourite firework display here.

A hundred years ago, was a favourite place for ballooning.

CONSTITUTION HILL

VICTORIA

THE QUEEN'S GALLERY

The Royal Standard is flown when the Queen is at Buckingham Palace. If not, she may be at Windsor Castle, Sandringham, Holyroodhouse or Balmoral.

Members of the royal family wave from the balcony on important occasions.

Charles II kept aviaries of exotic birds along here.

WELLINGTON BARRACKS

Changing of the Guard takes place here.

QUEEN VICTORIA MEMORIAL

CLARENCE HOUSE

BIRDCAGE WALK

Q. How many monarchs have lived at Buckingham Palace?

PLAYGROUND

W.C. FOR UNDER 11s

St. JAMES'S PARK

Once a marsh where pigs roamed, Charles II made this a park where he and his courtiers had fun. Today there is music, exotic wildfowl, lawns to play on and a good restaurant.

ST. JAMES'S PARK

The band plays here lunchtimes and early evenings June–September.

W.C.

THE MALL

ST. JAMES'S PALACE

QUEEN'S CHAPEL

George III, Victoria, Edward VIII, George V, Edward VIII, Elizabeth II

From the bridge you can see Big Ben and lots of fairytale towers (in fact they're just offices.)

Pelicans here are descended from the ones given to Charles II by the Russian Ambassador.

You can hire a deckchair here.

MARLBOROUGH HOUSE

Queen Anne, who at St. James's palace invited her best friend The Duchess of Marlborough to build her ma next door.

THE CAKE HOUSE

W E S N

BUCKINGHAM PALACE

This is the most recent royal London home. George III bought Buckingham House in 1762. George IV thought the house not nearly grand enough for a king. He began rebuilding it but ran out of money. Queen Victoria completed it and moved the great arch to Marble Arch. Queen Elizabeth II lives in about 12 of the 600 rooms, which include a private cinema and indoor swimming pool. Her bow-windowed sitting room overlooks Green Park (where bagpipes are played every morning during breakfast). The Royal Standard flies above the palace when the Queen is in residence, the Union Flag when she is not.

Three bits of Buckingham Palace to visit ~
1. *THE STATE ROOMS ~ including the throne.*
2. *THE QUEEN'S GALLERY ~ treasures from her art collection, one of the world's biggest.*
3. *THE ROYAL MEWS ~ see the State and Glass coaches and a sumptuous array of harnesses*

The Changing of the Guard

Since Charles II's restoration to the throne in 1660, the Household Division has protected the sovereign. It consists of the Household Cavalry and five Foot Guard regiments. Foot Guards guard Buckingham Palace.

Guard-mounting takes place at four London palaces:
BUCKINGHAM PALACE (the Queen's residence)
ST JAMES'S PALACE (the official court palace)
HORSEGUARDS ARCH (opposite the previous palace, Whitehall)
THE TOWER OF LONDON (the royal fortress)

Buckingham and St James's Palace combine their guard-mounting. At 11 am the old guard forms up in Friary Court, St James's Palace, and marches to music to Buckingham Palace. (Follow the dots on the map.) The new guard arrives from Wellington Barracks. Music plays while the guards march and the captains symbolically exchange keys. Meanwhile the sentries change at both palaces.

St James's Palace

Henry VIII built a hunting lodge here – his Gatehouse and clock survive. When Whitehall Palace burnt down in 1698, St James's became the principal royal London home until the move to Buckingham Palace. Charles II laid out St James's Park. He and his friends swam in the lake and played *pell-mell*, a French game similar to croquet. Today St James's Palace is still the official royal residence, even though the real one is Buckingham Palace.

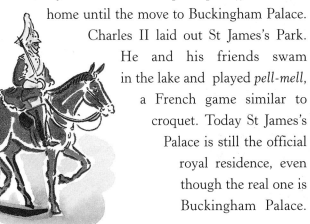

How to know which Foot Guard is marching ~
GRENADIER ~ white plume on left of bearskin: tunic buttons evenly spaced.
COLDSTREAM ~ scarlet plume on right of bearskin. Tunic buttons in pairs.
IRISH ~ pale blue plume on right of bearskin; buttons grouped in fours, and their Irish wolfhound mascot often leads them.
SCOTS ~ no bearskin plume: buttons grouped in threes.
WELSH ~ white and green plume on left of bearskin; buttons grouped in fives.

Q. How many years has Elizabeth II been Queen?

A. She was crowned on June 2 1953 but succeeded to the throne in 1952 when George VI died.

HAMPTON COURT PALACE

This is the BEST ROYAL PALACE to visit in London

Henry VIII took over Hampton Court Palace from Cardinal Thomas Wolsey in 1529. (The cardinal was in disgrace for failing to win Henry a divorce from his first wife.) Henry made it into one of Europe's grandest palaces. He began 400 years of splendour there. Elizabeth I and Charles II added to it. William III and Mary II, who reigned jointly, replaced a whole chunk; the Georgian kings added cosy rooms. And all the monarchs enjoyed 60 acres of formal gardens and the 2,000 acres of the two adjoining parks.

When the king and queen and their court came to stay, there were 1,000 people to feed and entertain. Henry built 50 kitchen rooms where 200 people prepared food for the 800 courtiers and servants he had to feed. In the Great Kitchen you can see a boar being roasted. They also ate peacock pie, venison from the parks and carp from the fishponds.

I was Prince of Orange in Holland before becoming William III of England in 1689. My wife and I dislike the London filth and dirty air, so we live at Kensington Palace and here. Christopher Wren, who is building St Paul's Cathedral, is making new rooms for us overlooking the formal gardens. It will be just like Versailles in France.

The Maze

Since 1838 visitors have replaced courtiers. The Maze is essential to see, but do look at some rooms, too. And don't miss Henry's kitchen. The whole palace, gardens and parks are there for you to explore.

Some of Wolsey's rooms, built 1515-1526, overlook Henry's Pond Gardens. Some of the Queen's pictures hang here, including one of Henry meeting the King of France on the Field of the Cloth of Gold.

Can you see Nicholas Orsain's Astronomical Clock made for Henry VIII in 1540? It is in the Wolsey Gateway in Clock Court. It shows the sun moving around the Earth!

Elizabeth I made this palace famous for good parties, feasts and theatre. When James succeeded her, Shakespeare acted in some of the 30 plays performed in the Great Hall at Christmas 1603.

Q. How many royal London palaces – whole or bits of them – can you visit?

A • Eight. They are: Buckingham Palace, the Tower of London, the Palace of Westminster (Westminster Hall and the Jewel Tower), Whitehall Palace, Kensington Palace, Greenwich (Queen's House), Kew Palace (and Queen Charlotte's Cottage) and St James's Palace (Friary Court and the Chapel).

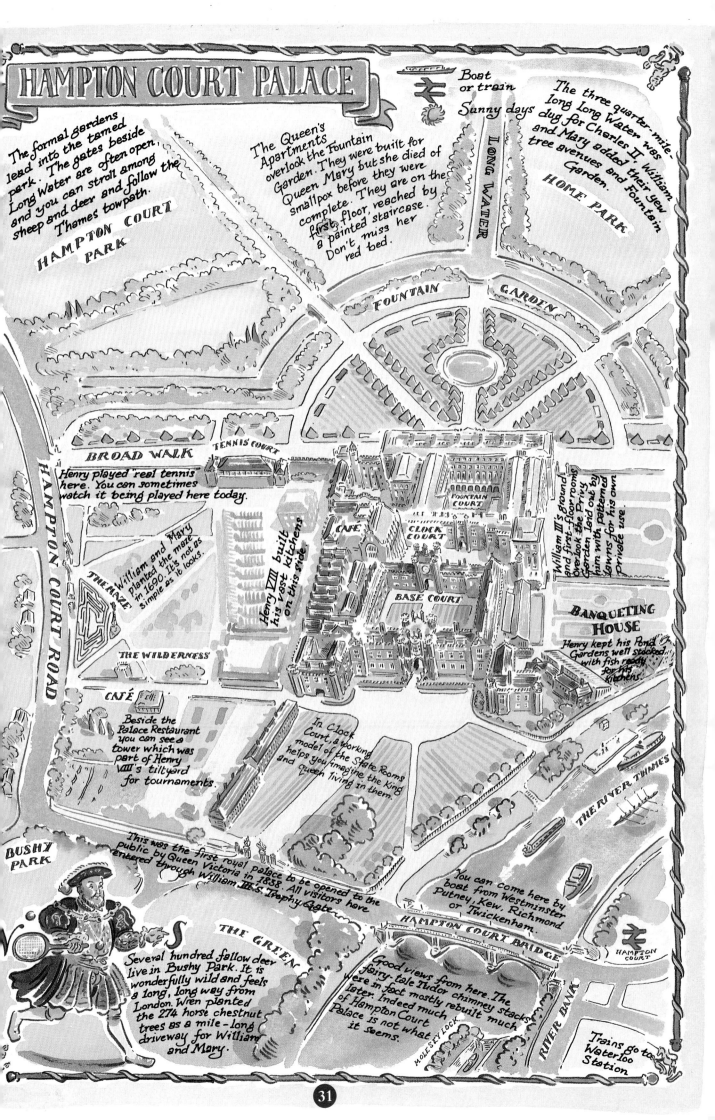

Boat or train

Sunny days

The three quarter-mile-long Long Water was dug for Charles II. William and Mary added their yew tree avenues and Fountain Garden.

The formal gardens lead into the tamed park. The gates beside Long Water are often open, and you can stroll among the sheep and deer and follow the Thames towpath.

HAMPTON COURT PARK

The Queen's Apartments overlook the Fountain Garden. They were built for Queen Mary but she died of smallpox before they were complete. They are on the first floor, reached by a painted staircase. Don't miss her red bed.

LONG WATER

HOME PARK

FOUNTAIN GARDEN

BROAD WALK

TENNIS COURT

Henry played 'real tennis' here. You can sometimes watch it being played here today.

THE MAZE

William and Mary planted the maze in 1690. It's not as simple as it looks.

Henry VIII built his vast kitchens on this side.

CAFÉ

FOUNTAIN COURT

CLOCK COURT

William III's ground and first-floor rooms overlook the Privy Garden laid out by him with patterned lawns for his own private use.

BASE COURT

BANQUETING HOUSE

Henry kept his Pond Gardens well stocked with fish ready for his kitchens.

THE WILDERNESS

CAFÉ

Beside the Palace Restaurant you can see a tower which was part of Henry VIII's tiltyard for tournaments.

In Clock Court, a working model of the State Rooms helps you imagine the King and Queen living in them.

HAMPTON COURT ROAD

BUSHY PARK

This was the first royal palace to be opened to the public by Queen Victoria in 1838. All visitors have entered through William III's Trophy Gate.

THE RIVER THAMES

You can come here by boat from Westminster, Putney, Kew, Richmond or Twickenham.

THE GREEN

HAMPTON COURT BRIDGE

HAMPTON COURT

Several hundred fallow deer live in Bushy Park. It is wonderfully wild and feels a long, long way from London. Wren planted the 274 horse chestnut trees as a mile-long driveway for William and Mary.

Good views from here. The fairy-tale Tudor chimney stacks were in fact mostly rebuilt much later. Indeed much of Hampton Court Palace is not what it seems.

MOLESEY LOCK

RIVER BANK

Trains go to Waterloo Station

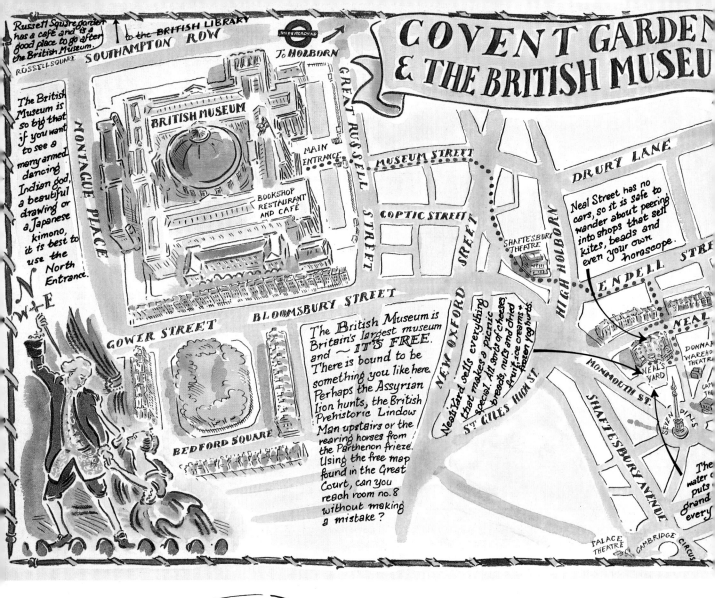

I am David Garrick, an actor and theatre manager living and working in Covent Garden in the eighteenth century. I put on Shakespeare's plays at the Theatre Royal Drury Lane, and give myself the best parts! Pulchinella (Mr Punch) gave his first London show in the Piazza in 1662. You can watch Punch and Judy here today and your sharp eyes can spot more than 15 theatres in the lanes.

Not long ago, Covent Garden was London's flower, fruit and vegetable market. The surrounding lanes became London's entertainment centre, both indoors and on the streets, for plenty of gambling, brawls and more sinister crimes took place there, too. Today, the old market halls are filled with shops, stalls and restaurants. They are great fun to explore; some roads are pedestrianised, and there is still plenty of street entertainment. For a change of pace, the British Museum is in nearby Bloomsbury.

London's Squares

Covent Garden Piazza was London's first square. People lived in houses along the sides. Later squares had gardens in the middle. In the squares around the British Museum you can see how Londoners lived. Householders rode in carriages to their front doors, while most tradesmen delivered to the back doors in the mews or a back lane. Coal, however, was delivered to the front of the house and the sacks emptied down coal holes, which you can still see on the pavements. They have circular covers.

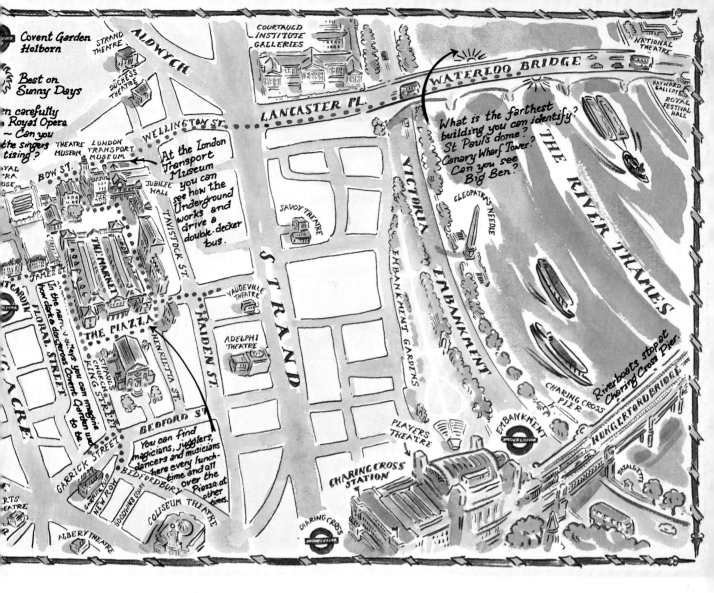

The Bow Street Runners

Two hundred and fifty years ago, Covent Garden was so full of robbers that this special group of thief-catchers worked here. So no one would spot them, they wore no uniform. They were paid reward money for every thief caught.

A Good Day Out
•••••••• follow the dots...

Start at the British Museum, then explore the alleys, lanes and shops of Covent Garden, have a picnic in the Piazza watching entertainers, check out the London Transport Museum and see how much you can see from Waterloo Bridge. Some of the shops sell amazing things. Try to find the theatrical make-up shop in Tavistock St, the bead and kite shops in Neal St, the candle shop in the Market and the rubber stamp shop in Neal's Yard.

If it Rains...

◊ **THE LONDON TRANSPORT MUSEUM** tells us the story of the world's largest urban transport system which carries more than 6,500,000 passengers a day more than 500,000 miles.

◊ **THE THEATRE MUSEUM** is the National Museum of Performing Arts, including puppetry and the circus.

◊ **THE COURTAULD INSTITUTE GALLERIES** have wonderful Impressionist paintings hung in grand and beautiful rooms.

◊ **THE BRITISH LIBRARY** five minutes walk north from the British Museum, displays the Magna Carta, tells the story of books and lets you design one yourself.

AND There's the **BRITISH MUSEUM**

Q. Can you guess the origin of Covent Garden?

A. It was a convent garden belonging to Westminster Abbey.

REGENT'S PARK

The Regent was King George III's son, Prince George. He became Regent (ruler) in 1811 when his father went insane. He became King George IV when his father died in 1820.

The Prince Regent wanted London to look as elegant as Paris. With his architect, John Nash, he laid out all of Regent Street, Regent's Park and the terraces around it.

Regent's Park was designed to be a garden dotted with 56 country villas, but only eight villas were built (and only three still stand).

Today it is one of ten Royal Parks in London. The others are Bushy, Green, Greenwich, Hampton Court, Hyde, Kensington Gardens, Primrose Hill, Richmond and St James's.

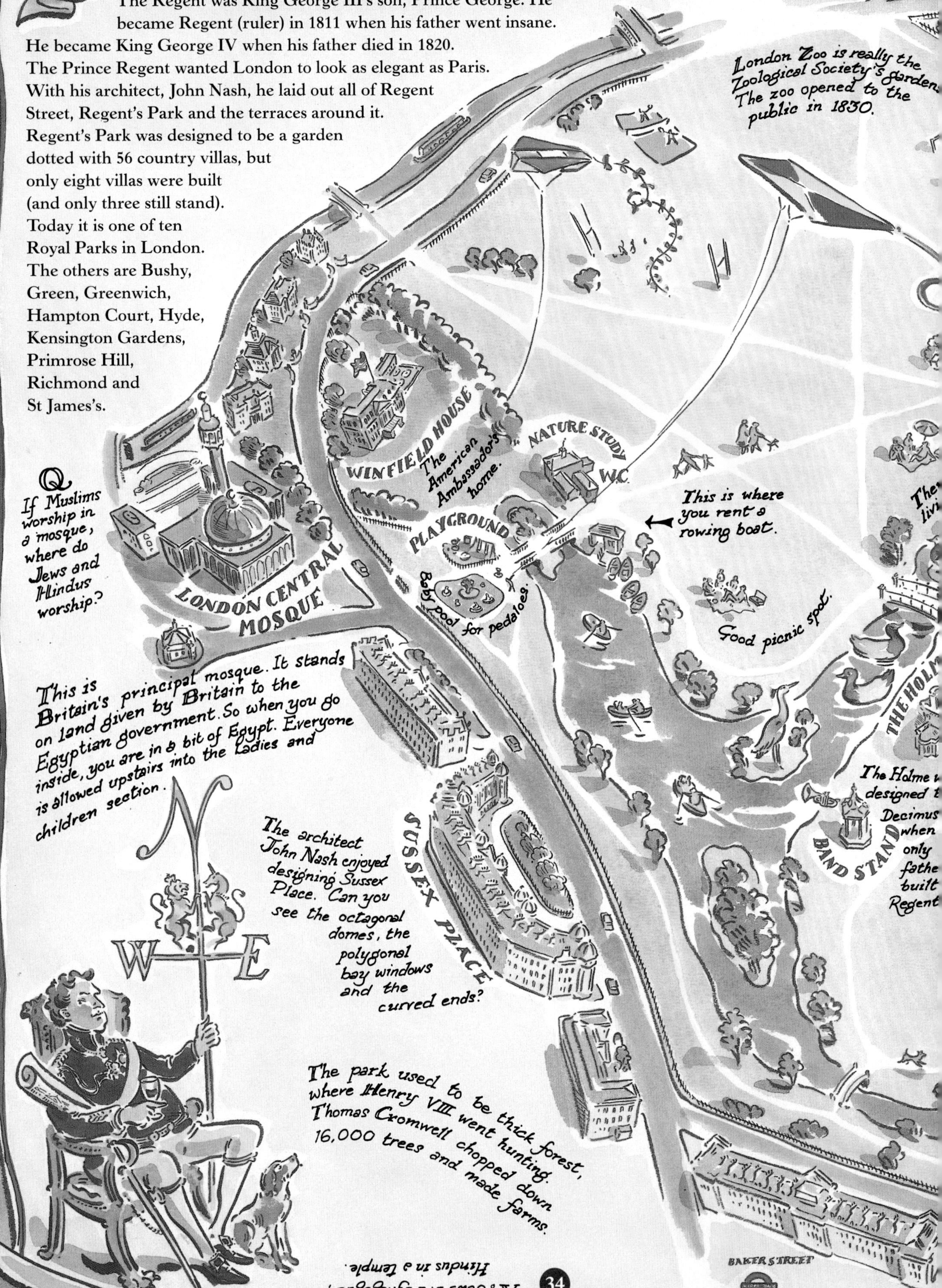

London Zoo is really the Zoological Society's garden. The zoo opened to the public in 1830.

Q If Muslims worship in a mosque, where do Jews and Hindus worship?

WINFIELD HOUSE

The American Ambassador's home.

NATURE STUDY

W.C.

PLAYGROUND

Baby pool for pedaloes.

This is where you rent a rowing boat.

Good picnic spot.

LONDON CENTRAL MOSQUE

This is Britain's principal mosque. It stands on land given by Britain to the Egyptian government. So when you go inside, you are in a bit of Egypt. Everyone is allowed upstairs into the Ladies and children section.

THE HOLM

The Holme was designed by Decimus when only father built Regent

BAND STAND

The architect John Nash enjoyed designing Sussex Place. Can you see the octagonal domes, the polygonal bay windows and the curved ends?

SUSSEX PLACE

The park used to be thick forest, where Henry VIII went hunting. Thomas Cromwell chopped down 16,000 trees and made farms.

W E

BAKER STREET

A. Jews in a synagogue, Hindus in a temple.

34

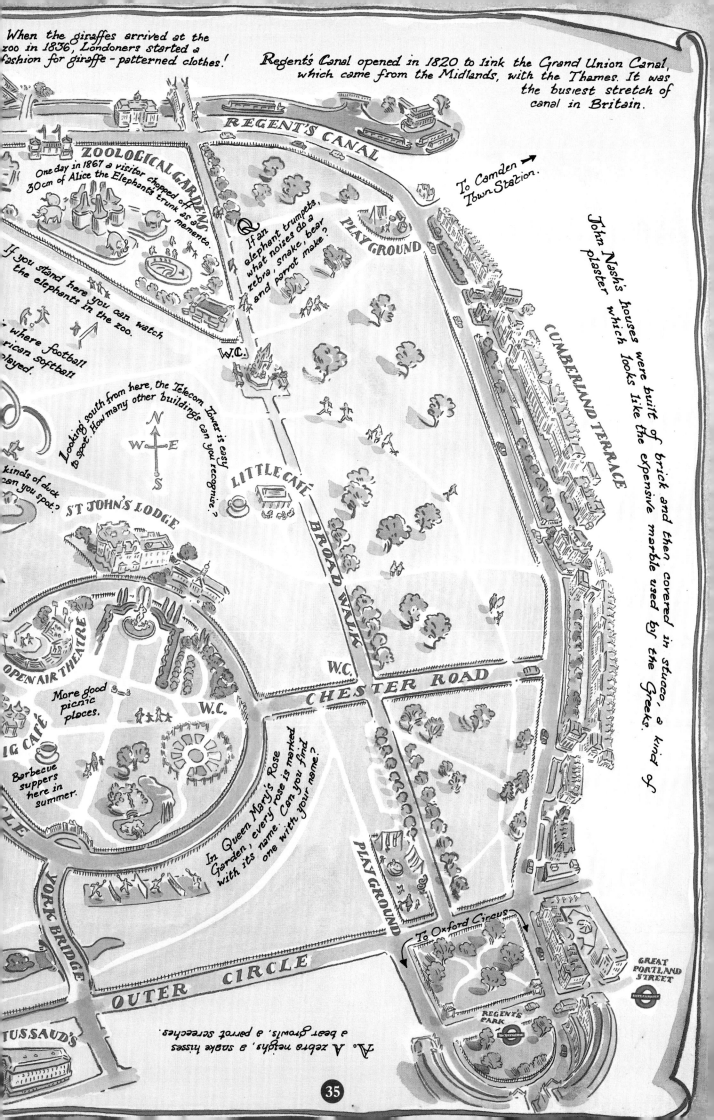

When the giraffes arrived at the zoo in 1836, Londoners started a fashion for giraffe-patterned clothes!

Regent's Canal opened in 1820 to link the Grand Union Canal, which came from the Midlands, with the Thames. It was the busiest stretch of canal in Britain.

REGENT'S CANAL

ZOOLOGICAL GARDENS

One day in 1867 a visitor chopped off 30cm of Alice the Elephant's trunk as a memento.

To Camden Town Station.

If an elephant trumpets, what noises do a zebra, snake, bear and parrot make?

PLAY GROUND

If you stand here you can watch the elephants in the zoo.

W.C.

where football ...rican softball ...layed.

John Nash's houses were built of brick and then covered in stucco, a kind of plaster which looks like the expensive marble used by the Greeks.

CUMBERLAND TERRACE

Looking south from here, the Telecom Tower is easy to spot. How many other buildings can you recognise?

N
W + E
S

LITTLE CAFE

kinds of duck can you spot.

ST JOHN'S LODGE

BROAD WALK

W.C.

CHESTER ROAD

OPEN AIR THEATRE

More good picnic places.

W.C.

...G CAFE

Barbecue suppers here in summer.

In Queen Mary's Rose Garden, every rose is marked with its name. Can you find one with your name?

PLAYGROUND

To Oxford Circus

...CLE

YORK BRIDGE

OUTER CIRCLE

...TUSSAUD'S

A. A zebra neighs, a snake hisses a bear growls, a parrot screeches.

REGENT'S PARK

GREAT PORTLAND STREET

35

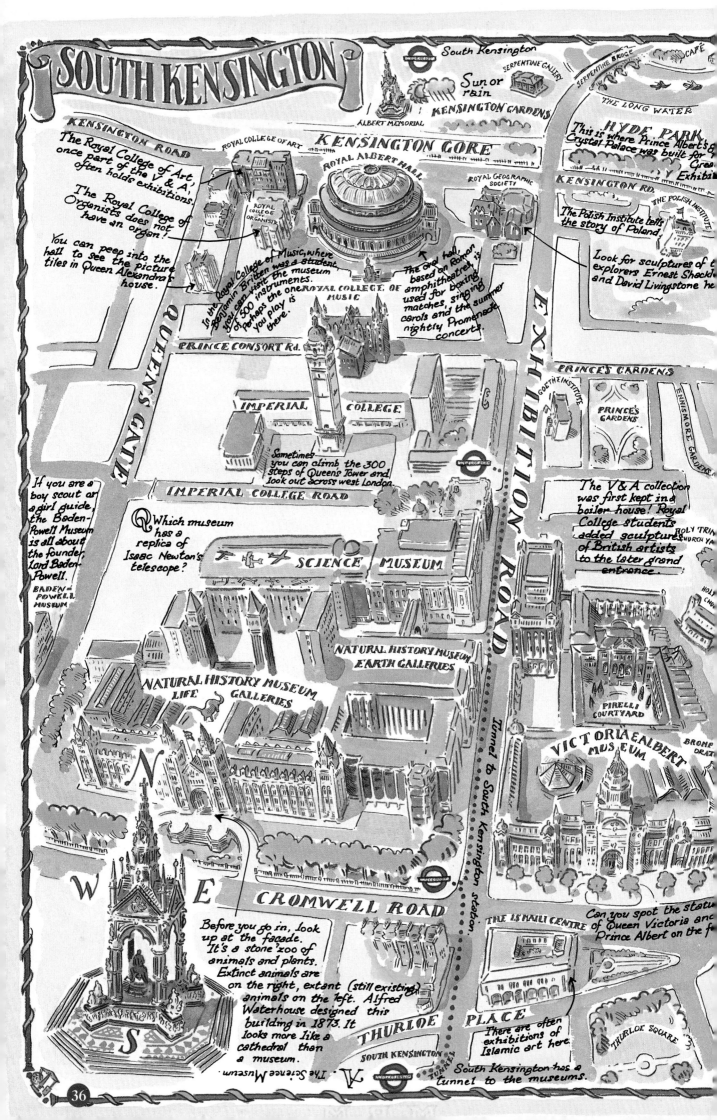

SOUTH KENSINGTON

South Kensington

Sun or rain

SERPENTINE GALLERY

SERPENTINE BRIDGE   CAFÉ

THE LONG WATER

ALBERT MEMORIAL

KENSINGTON GARDENS

HYDE PARK
This is where Prince Albert's Crystal Palace was built for Great Exhibition

KENSINGTON ROAD

The Royal College of Art, once part of the V & A, often holds exhibitions.

ROYAL COLLEGE OF ART

KENSINGTON GORE

ROYAL ALBERT HALL

ROYAL GEOGRAPHIC SOCIETY

KENSINGTON RD.

THE POLISH INSTITUTE

The Royal College of Organists does not have an organ!

ROYAL COLLEGE ORGANIST

The Polish Institute tells the story of Poland.

You can peep into the hall to see the picture tiles in Queen Alexandra's house.

In the Royal College of Music, where Benjamin Britten was a student, you can visit the museum of 500 instruments. Perhaps the one you play is there.

ROYAL COLLEGE OF MUSIC

The oval hall, based on Roman amphitheatres, is used for boxing matches, singing carols and the summer nightly Promenade concerts.

Look for sculptures of the explorers Ernest Shackleton and David Livingstone here

PRINCE CONSORT Rd.

EXHIBITION ROAD

PRINCE'S GARDENS

GOETHE INSTITUTE

PRINCE'S GARDENS

ENNISMORE GARDENS

IMPERIAL COLLEGE

Sometimes you can climb the 300 steps of Queen's Tower and look out across west London.

IMPERIAL COLLEGE ROAD

The V&A collection was first kept in a boiler house! Royal College students added sculptures of British artists to the later grand entrance.

HOLY TRINITY CHURCH YARD

If you are a boy scout or a girl guide, the Baden-Powell Museum is all about the founder, Lord Baden-Powell.

BADEN-POWELL MUSEUM

Q Which museum has a replica of Isaac Newton's telescope?

SCIENCE MUSEUM

HOLY CHO...

NATURAL HISTORY MUSEUM EARTH GALLERIES

PIRELLI COURTYARD

NATURAL HISTORY MUSEUM LIFE GALLERIES

VICTORIA & ALBERT MUSEUM

BROMP... ORAT...

N

W   E   S

Tunnel to South Kensington station.

CROMWELL ROAD

THE ISMAILI CENTRE

Can you spot the statues of Queen Victoria and Prince Albert on the fa...

Before you go in, look up at the facade. It's a stone 'zoo' of animals and plants. Extinct animals are on the right, extant (still existing) animals on the left. Alfred Waterhouse designed this building in 1873. It looks more like a cathedral than a museum.

THURLOE PLACE

There are often exhibitions of Islamic art here.

THURLOE SQUARE

The Science Museum

SOUTH KENSINGTON

South Kensington has a tunnel to the museums.

TUNNEL

36

SOUTH KENSINGTON

The museums of South Kensington are really a giant indoor playground for endless discovery – for finding out how a whale lives, what the Earth is made of, how a car works or what people eat with in Japan.

HOT TIP ①

Children under 16 have free entry to all three museums at all times. Children under 14 must be accompanied by an adult.

HOT TIP ②

The information desks usually have projects for children.

HOT TIP ③

Famous rooms in the big museums get crowded. Others, especially on higher floors, do not, and are just as interesting.

HOT TIP ④

Take some drinks or fruit in a backpack. The café is always far away when you are thirsty.

HOT TIP ⑤

It might be fun to drop into one of the smaller colleges or institutes surrounding the Big Three museums, taking a break in a park in between.

PRINCE ALBERT
I am Queen Victoria's husband, Prince Albert. The Great Exhibition I organised in 1851 was so good that one third of the whole population of Britain came. I used the profits towards building this museum village. You can explore some of the museums and then go and see my statue in Kensington Gardens. I'm holding the Great Exhibition catalogue and facing my village of discovery 'ALBERTOPOLIS.'

Inside the Big Three

The three big national museums are HUGE
Using the plans, it is best to choose just two or three galleries to seek out.

THE SCIENCE MUSEUM

as more than 200,000 items telling he stories of discoveries and inventions. They are in 70 galleries in five floors including the Space Gallery, where you can see the lunar module, Apollo 10, and the aeronautics Gallery where there are all sorts of real aeroplanes to look at. See if you can find out how a plastic bag is made and how a telephone works. The new Wellcome Wing has state-of the-art displays and an IMAX theatre.

THE NATURAL HISTORY MUSEUM

is in two parts.

THE EARTH GALLERIES tell the story of the Earth itself. You can see a 330-million-year-old fossil of a Scottish fern, or experience an earthquake and shake about, or push buttons to see which minerals are found in everyday objects, or what would happen if the climate changed.

THE LIFE GALLERIES show only some of their 50 million treasures which tell the story of life on Earth.

As well as the dinosaur rooms, try to find the human biology gallery and, upstairs, the Darwin room.

THE VICTORIA & ALBERT MUSEUM

known as the V & A, is like an encyclopaedia of the history of the world. Instead of words, it uses objects – perhaps a full-scale copy of Trajan's column in Rome, perhaps an Indian shawl, perhaps whole rooms from destroyed London buildings. Its 145 galleries joined end to end would be seven miles long; no one can count how many objects it contains. Prince Albert hoped the V & A would give people ideas for designing and inventing. See if you can make up a pattern or invent something useful from one of the objects on show. It could make you rich and famous!

RAINY DAYS

Rainy Day Outings

It doesn't always rain in London! But it often manages to rain just when you are off out on the town. The London Happiness Code says always have a **PLAN B** ready for when it rains, so here are five Plan Bs for keeping dry and still having London fun. All the places but one can be found on the **TEN BIG MAPS**

①

Go to *SOUTH KENSINGTON* (p. 36 - 37) and use the tunnel to reach the museum you want to visit.

②

See how London's vast transport system was built, at the *LONDON TRANSPORT MUSEUM* (p. 32 - 33) Then speed on to the Pepsi Trocadero for stomach-turning rides at Segaworld and the IMAX theatre.

③

Spend the day at the *BARBICAN CENTRE* (p. 20 - 21). There is the Museum of London, The Barbican Art Gallery, two cinemas, a concert hall and two Royal Shakespeare Company theatres, which sometimes have matiné shows, and lots of free events for children, especially during school holidays.

④

Spend the day at the *BRITISH MUSEUM* (p. 32 - 33), Britain's largest museum. Start in the Great Court, to collect a map and find out what special events and exhibitions are on. Then find the Egyptian mummies, learn about London in Roman times and look for the dancing Hindu god, Shiva, in room 33.

⑤

Explore London's biggest and best toy department and perhaps buy something at *HARRODS* in Knightsbridge (east of the map on p. 36 - 37), where TOY KINGDOM is on the 4th floor.

⑥

If you can't play football, see all your heroes in the *FOOTBALL HALL OF FAME*.

Museums for You

Here are some more museums which are especially interesting for children and may well have events or workshop

☆ *THE LONDON AQUARIUM* has huge tanks of all kinds of weird and wonderful fish. Don't miss feeding time for the sharks, the touching pool full of rays, or the excellent shop.

★ **THE BBC EXPERIENCE** is in the BBC's headquarters, in Portland Place. During your tour you can act in a radio play, commentate a football game, and read the weather forecast on TV.

☆ Bethnal Green *MUSEUM of CHILDHOOD* Cambridge Heath Road, E2: an outpost of the V & A, this ol train-shed is packed with toys old and new, from an estate of dolls' houses to elaborate trainsets and a comple model of a circus. Lots of holiday workshops.

☆ *POLLOCK'S TOY MUSEUM* 1 Scala St, W1: two London houses crammed with old toys, and an excellent shop which sells Benjamin Pollock's toy theatres, puppets and lots of other rainy-day activities.

★ *IMPERIAL WAR MUSEUM* Lambeth Road, SE1: experience the trenches, see what would happen if nuclear bomb hit London, and use hands-on exhibits to explore the atrocities and reasons for war.

Rainy Day Sports

Splash about indoors!

When the parks and playgrounds are off limits during a downpour, London has plenty of indoor sports, especially swimming. Here are a few ideas:

✦ KIDZ CLUB

at London Central YMCA, 112 Great Russell St, WC1: swimming, climbing, trampolining and more, every Saturday 10 am - noon.
Adult members can also take children swimming at weekends, noon - 5 pm.

✦ ARCHWAY POOL

McDonald Road, N19: open for children 3.30 - 6.30 pm weekdays, all day at weekends. The large leisure pool has wave sessions and a river run.

✦ QUEEN MOTHER SPORTS CENTRE

228 Vauxhall Bridge Rd, SW1: three swimming pools plus archery, badminton, table tennis, trampolining and more.

✦ QUEENS ICE SKATING CLUB

Queens Court, Queensway, W2: open to all every day with skates available for hire.

or.... Sit back and be entertained with

Theatre

Some theatres have matinée shows, where tickets are often cheaper than for the evening performance. Also, the Half Price Ticket Booth in Leicester Square sells matinée tickets from noon, evening tickets from 2.30 pm.

London has some very lively children's theatres. Most have morning and afternoon shows at weekends, fewer shows on weekdays.

✦ LITTLE ANGEL MARIONETTE THEATRE
14 Dagmar Passage, Cross St, N1.

✦ POLKA THEATRE FOR CHILDREN
240 The Broadway, Wimbledon, SW19.

✦ UNICORN THEATRE FOR CHILDREN
6 - 7 Great Newport St, WC2.

In addition, there are often special children's shows at these theatres: Lyric, Hammersmith; Riverside Studios; Sadler's Wells (which stages lots of dance); Tricycle Theatre.

Music

The South Bank Centre has regular concerts for children in their three halls: Royal Festival Hall, Queen Elizabeth Hall and the Purcell Room.
The wonderful programme of Ernest Read Concerts for Children takes place in the the Royal Festival Hall. Ring 0207 960 4242 for details.

A Good Film

You can watch the latest blockbusters on big screens in Leicester Square cinemas. There are also special children's programmes:

✦ THE NATIONAL FILM THEATRE
at the South Bank, screens Junior NFT films at weekends, around 4pm (no membership needed).

✦ IMAX THEATRES
in the Pepsi Trocadero, the Science Museum and the London IMAX at the South Bank offer you a thrilling virtual experience.

✦ BARBICAN CHILDREN'S CINEMA CLUB
at the Barbican Centre. You need to enrol as a member to see the regular Saturday film at 11 am.

... and if you STILL do not know what to do when it rains... phone VISITORCALL or KIDSLINE (p. 8) or comb through the pages of *Time Out*.

HOME GAMES

Here are some **LONDON GAMES** to play while you are exploring.

London Trivia

Test yourself and your friends on these questions about London. The answers are on page 44. You might find out more by asking the guides these questions when you are out and about.

1. Which was London's first bridge across the Thames?

2. What is Big Ben?

3. What does Trafalgar Square commemorate?

4. Which king did the Prince Regent become?

5. In 1836, London's first railway ran four miles between which stations?

6. Where is the Rosetta Stone?

7. What happened on September 2, 1666?

8. To go from Westminster Abbey to the Tate Modern, which direction would you travel?

9. In the nursery rhyme 'Two little dickie birds sitting on a wall, one named Peter, the other named Paul', who are Peter and Paul?

10. Is the Tower of London upstream or downstream of Tower Bridge?

London Forfeits

This is an action game for two or more players. All you need is a pair of dice. First, using the **TEN BIG MAPS**, write down some forfeits about the places you have visited on pieces of paper and fold them up. Here are a few ideas:

PRETEND TO WALK UP ALL 530 STEPS TO THE VERY TOP OF ST PAUL'S.

☆

GIVE DIRECTIONS FOR GETTING FROM BUCKINGHAM PALACE TO TRAFALGAR SQUARE.

☆

YOU ARE ONE OF HENRY VIII's WIVES RECENTLY EXECUTED. LIE DEAD UNTIL YOUR NEXT TURN.

☆

IMITATE A LONDON BEEFEATER AND GIVE AN IMAGINARY TOUR OF THE TOWER OF LONDON FOR ONE MINUTE.

To Play:

Players take it in turns to throw the dice. When a player throws a double, he or she must act out a forfeit.

Postcard Jigsaw

Buy a jumbo-sized picture postcard on one of your visits. On the back draw very wavy lines across it horizontally and vertically, then cut along them to make a jigsaw. The smaller the pieces, the harder the jigsaw. Make a really difficult puzzle from a collage of tickets from your travels stuck on to a piece of card.

MORE LONDON GAMES

There are all sorts of well-known games that you can adapt to a London theme. Here are some ideas:

★ CHARADES

Two teams take it in turns to guess what London subject the other is miming, e.g.: The Great Fire; Changing of the Guard; Animals in the zoo; Boudicca in her chariot; and so on.

☆ PICTURE GAME

Teams take it in turns to draw a London subject. One team chooses the subject. The other team chooses a drawer, who is not allowed to speak whilst drawing. The team has to guess what it is within one minute to gain a point. Change the drawer each time. Ideas: Tower Bridge, newspaper vendor, the Millennium Dome.

☆ TELL ~ A ~ STORY

The first player gives three London words or phrases to the second, who must use them all to make up a story set in London. The second player then gives three more to the next, who continues the story. You could try with some of these: Prince Albert, black taxi, travelcard, the front seat upstairs on a bus, two pigeons, a red letterbox, etc.

☆ SNAKES AND LADDERS

Draw out your own Snakes and Ladders board. Put six London disasters at the tops of the snakes (such as getting stuck in a traffic jam, turning up when a tourist attraction is closed, train strike, etc.) and six pieces of good news for Londoners at the bottoms of the ladders (such as being first in the queue for a popular event, remembering to bring a drink and food with you, getting somewhere quickly by Underground, etc.). Then play your game with dice as you would play Snakes and Ladders.

★ NAME GAME

Take it in turns to think of a London name starting with the last letter of the previous word. For example: the first player kicks off with Regent's ParK; the second follows with KnightsbridgE; the third with Elephant and CastlE (another E, oh dear) and so on. Tip: Underground stations are very useful in this game.

Monopoly

Playing Monopoly is a good reminder of London street names. Now try finding these 'properties' in a London street atlas and look out for them when you are travelling around.

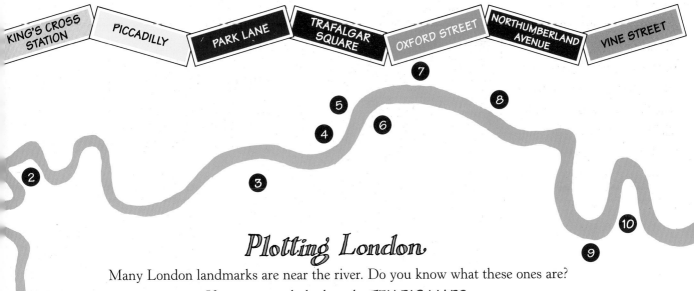

Plotting London

Many London landmarks are near the river. Do you know what these ones are?
If you get stuck, look at the TEN BIG MAPS.

AWAY GAMES

*Here are some **LONDON GAMES** to play while you are exploring*

Double~Decker I~Spy

Who can be the first to spot these TEN things from the top of a bus?

ANOTHER RED BUS
Spotted by :

A PUBLIC CLOCK
Spotted by :

A SHOP WITH 'BY ROYAL APPOINTMENT' ARMS
Spotted by :

A CHURCH
Spotted by :

A ZEBRA CROSSING
Spotted by :

AN UNDERGROUND STATION
Spotted by :

A TAXI
Spotted by :

A UNION JACK
Spotted by :

A FIRE STATION
Spotted by :

A WEATHER VANE
Spotted by :

THE WINNER:

Look Out Londoners!

✓ Tick off these Londoners as you see them:

- [ ] A NEWS VENDOR
- [ ] A MOUNTED POLICE OFFICER
- [ ] A RIVER POLICE OFFICER
- [ ] A BEEFEATER
- [ ] A TRAFFIC WARDEN
- [ ] A HOT-CHESTNUT VENDOR (or ICE-CREAM VENDOR in summer)
- [ ] A HOTEL DOORMAN
- [ ] A TAXI DRIVER
- [ ] A BICYCLE COURIER
- [ ] A SENTRY

Streetwise

✓ Look out for these things in the streets:

- [ ] A PUB SIGN
- [ ] A COAL-HOLE COVER
- [ ] A RED TELEPHONE BOX
- [ ] A FULL-LENGTH STATUE
- [ ] A DECORATED LAMP POST
- [ ] A HOUSE WITH A BLUE PLAQUE (where someone famous once lived)
- [ ] A DOORWAY WITH A FANLIGHT
- [ ] A RED LETTERBOX
- [ ] DECORATIVE TILES on a path or shop front
- [ ] A HOIST POLE sticking out from the front of a building

Bird's~Eye London

Look out for these landmarks when you are at the top of a building such as St Paul's, the Monument or Tower Bridge, or when you are on the higher terraces of the National Theatre or at Greenwich Park:

☐ CANARY WHARF

☐ THE THAMES

☐ MILLENNIUM DOME

☐ NELSON'S COLUMN

☐ THE TOWER OF LONDON AND TOWER BRIDGE

☐ BRITISH AIRWAYS LONDON EYE

☐ BIG BEN

☐ ST PAUL'S CATHEDRAL

Scavengers

Some of the best souvenirs are the ones that you don't buy in the tourist shops. See if everyone in your party can find these things for a scavenger hunt, or just collect them anyway and keep them (or some of them) in a scrapbook:

PIGEON FEATHER

PLANE TREE LEAF

LONDON NEWSPAPER

A FLYER FOR SOME EVENT

BUS TICKET

A BUS OR TUBE MAP

COASTER, BEER-MAT OR PAPER NAPKIN
(from somewhere you've had a meal)

PENCIL FROM A MUSEUM OR GALLERY SHOP

A 2p PIECE

A CARRIER BAG FROM A FAMOUS STORE

POSTCARDS FROM AN ART GALLERY

A LEAFLET FROM A MUSEUM

PHOTO OF YOURSELF WITH A POLICEMAN

Look Sharp!

Find the answers to these questions.

1. Who is riding a horse in St Paul's Cathedral?

Answer :

2. What is on top of the Monument?

Answer :

3. Which arm did Nelson lose?

Answer :

4. Whose memorial is in front of Buckingham Palace?

Answer :

5. In what colours is the clock face of Big Ben painted?

Answer :

6. What is at either end of the Millennium Bridge?

Answer :

7. What is the statue at Piccadilly Circus?

Answer :

8. Who is riding a chariot on Westminster Bridge?

Answer :

9. What is on top of the lamp posts in the Mall?

Answer :

10. What famous child has a statue in Kensington Gardens?

Answer :

BIG BEN

How to make your own BIG BEN!

Cutting Out

is easy. Just follow the lines on the back. The more accurate your cutting, the better your model will be. To protect your book, you could make a double-sided colour copy of pages 45 and 46.

folding

is more tricky, as it must be exactly along the lines. For both sections, fold all the sticking flaps inwards fir then, following the FOLD IN and FOLD OUT directions, create the shape of each piece.

Sticking

is best done using a glue stick. First glue the clock, face by face, leaving the open sides until last, then glu the folded tower to the lower flaps of the clock, finally gluing the long sides of the tower.

Display

your BIG BEN MODEL on the back cover of LOOK OUT LONDON!

BIG BEN FACTS

Big Ben is just the name of the huge hour bell, although it has grown to be the nickname for the whole clock and St Stephen's Tower of the Houses of Parliament.

☆

Charles Barry designed the Clock Tower in 1844 to be the world's biggest and best. The tower is 97.5 metres high the clock faces are 7 metres in diameter, the hour hands 2.7 metres and the minute hands 4.2 metres. The clock was designed and made by E.J. Dent and is still very accurate today.

☆

The first Big Ben bell, delivered by boat from Stockton-on-Tees, cracked. The second, cast at Whitechapel in the East End of London in 1858, also cracked but only a little, so it was left. It weighs 13 tonnes.

☆

The clock's mechanism could not push round the heavy cast-iron hands so they were remade in lighter gun-metal, but the minute hand still fell several feet after it passed 12, so it was remade in hollow copper.

☆

Clock and bell went into operation on May 31, 1859 – and have kept Londoners on time ever since.

QUIZ Answers

LOOK SHARP

1. Duke of Wellington.
2. A bowl of flames.
3. His right arm.
4. Queen Victoria's.
5. Black and white.
6. St Paul's Cathedral and the Tate Modern.
7. 'The Angel of Christian Charity' – wrongly known as 'Eros'.
8. Boudicca.
9. Ships.
10. Peter Pan.

LONDON TRIVIA

1. London Bridge.
2. The hour bell of the clock in the Clock Tower of the Houses of Parliament.
3. The Battle of Trafalgar 1805, during which Admiral Lord Nelson died.
4. George IV.
5. London Bridge and Greenwich.
6. In the British Museum.
7. The Great Fire of London broke out at the bakery in Pudding Lane.
8. South.
9. The patron Saints of Westminster Abbey and St Paul's Cathedral.
10. Upstream.

PLOTTING LONDON

1. Hampton Court.
2. Kew Gardens.
3. Battersea Power Station.
4. Tate Britain.
5. Houses of Parliament.
6. South Bank Centre.
7. St Paul's Cathedral.
8. Tower of London.
9. Greenwich.
10. The Millennium Experience.

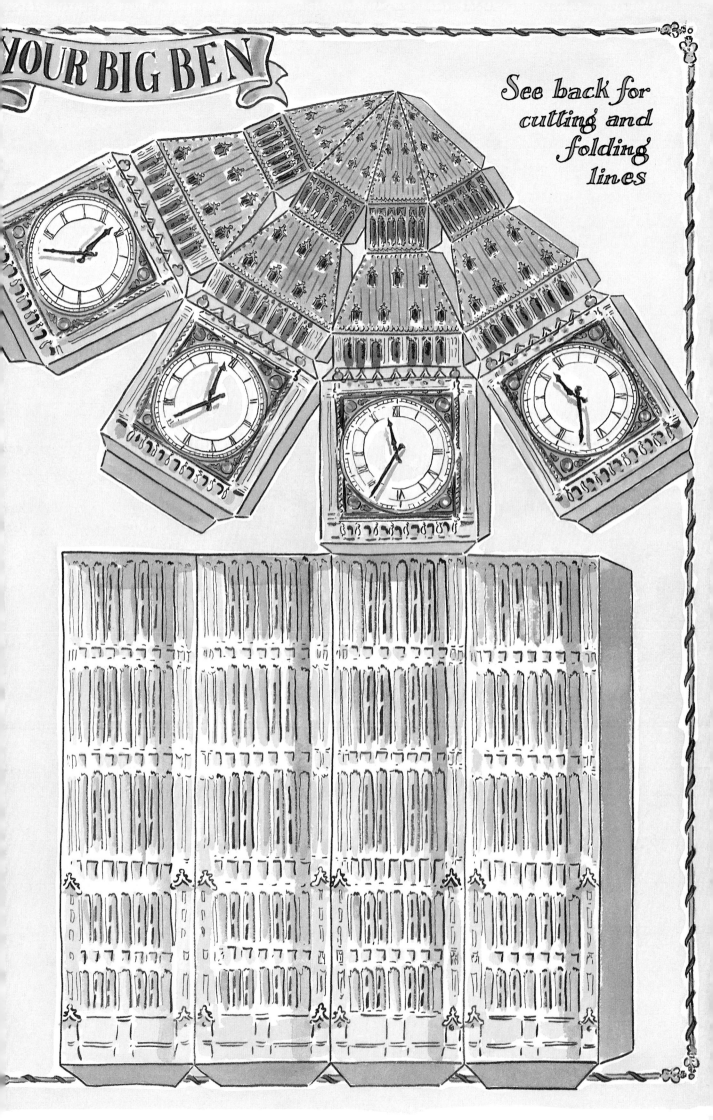

YOUR BIG BEN

See back for cutting and folding lines

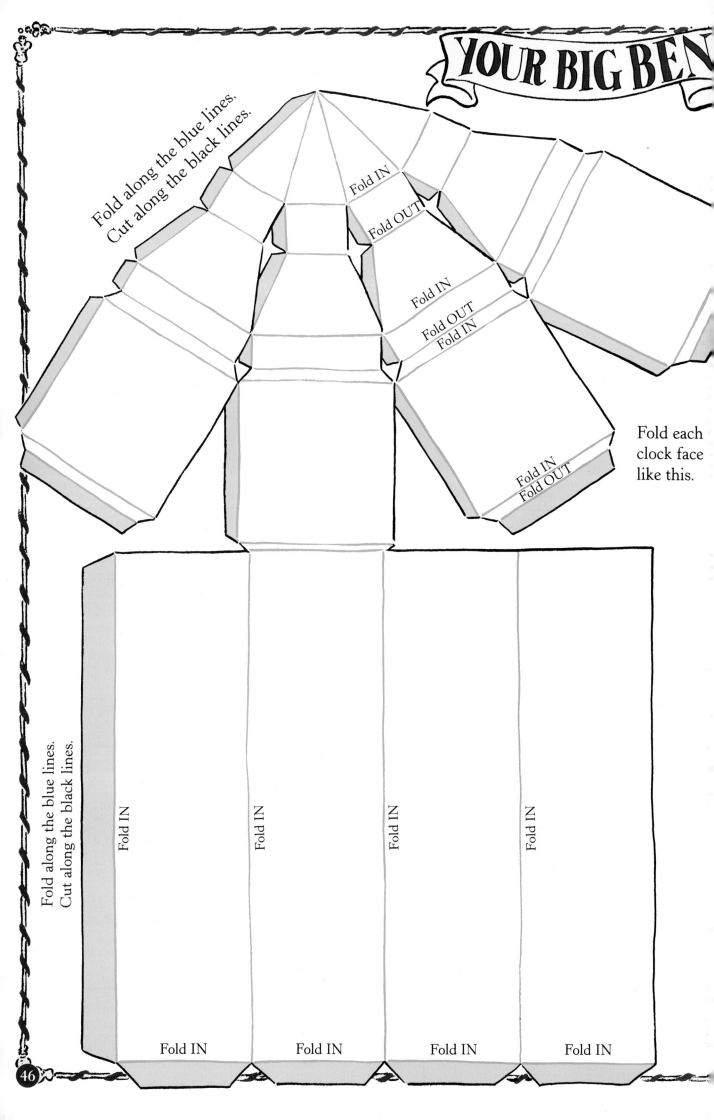

Fold along the blue lines.
Cut along the black lines.

Fold IN

Fold OUT

Fold IN

Fold OUT
Fold IN

Fold IN
Fold OUT

Fold each
clock face
like this.

Fold along the blue lines.
Cut along the black lines.

Fold IN

Fold IN

Fold IN

Fold IN

Fold IN

Fold IN

Fold IN

Fold IN

NDEX

HENRY VIII